❦ STRANGE TALES ❦
FROM
MANY LANDS

Edited by
Freya Littledale

Illustrated by Mila Lazarevich

Doubleday & Company, Inc., Garden City, New York

Grateful acknowledgment is made to the following for permission to reprint their copyrighted material:

DOUBLEDAY & COMPANY, INC. "The Bird that Would Not Stay Dead" from *African Wonder Tales* by Frances Carpenter. Copyright © 1963 by Frances Carpenter Huntington. Reprinted by permission of Doubleday & Company, Inc.

HOLT, RINEHART AND WINSTON, INC. "The Golden Cockerel," originally entitled "The Golden Cock" adapted from *Skazki: Tales and Legends of Old Russia* told by Ida Zeitlin. Copyright 1926 by Holt, Rinehart and Winston, Inc. Copyright 1954 by Ida Zeitlin Nadejen. Reprinted by permission of Holt, Rinehart and Winston, Inc.

ALFRED A. KNOPF, INC. "The Knight with the Stone Heart" from *The Three Sneezes and Other Swiss Tales*, by Roger Duvoisin. Copyright 1941 by Alfred A. Knopf, Inc. and renewed 1969 by Roger Duvoisin. Reprinted by permission of the publisher.

HELEN FINGER LEFLAR "El Enano" from *Tales from Silver Lands* by Charles Finger. Copyright 1924 by Doubleday & Company, Inc. Reprinted by permission of Helen Finger Leflar.

J. B. LIPPINCOTT COMPANY "The Inn that Wasn't There," originally entitled "The Night on the Battlefield" adapted from *The Chinese Fairy Book* by R. Welhelm. Translated by Frederick H. Martens. Copyright 1921 by Frederick A. Stokes Company. Copyright renewed 1949 by Herman C. Martens; "Tokutaro," originally entitled "Tokutaro San" from *Wonder Tales of Old Japan* by Bernard Henderson and C. Calvert. Published by Frederick A. Stokes Company (1924), and "The Seal Catcher and the Merman" from *The Scottish Fairy Book* by Elizabeth H. Grierson. Published by Frederick A. Stokes Company (1910). Reprinted by permission of J. B. Lippincott Company. All rights reserved.

NORRIS MODERN PRESS LIMITED "The Water-Bull," originally entitled "The Tarroo-Ushtey" from *Fairy Tales from the Isle of Man* by Dora Broome. Copyright 1951 by Dora Broome. Edited and reprinted by permission of Norris Modern Press Limited. All rights reserved.

THE VIKING PRESS, INC. "Tiger Woman" from *Which Was Witch?* by Eleanore M. Jewett. Copyright 1953 by Eleanore Myers Jewett. Reprinted by permission of The Viking Press, Inc.

HENRY Z. WALCK, INC. AND OXFORD UNIVERSITY PRESS "The Piper of Keil" "Richmuth of Cologne" from *German Hero-Sagas and Folk Tales* © by Barbara Leonie Picard 1954. Reprinted by permission of Henry Z. Walck, Inc., publishers, and Oxford University Press, London.

WESTERN PUBLISHING COMPANY, INC. "The Terrible Stranger" by Robert M. Hyatt from *Story Parade* copyright 1936, copyright renewed 1964 by Story Parade, Inc. Edited by permission of Western Publishing Company, Inc.

Library of Congress Cataloging in Publication Data

Littledale, Freya, 1929–   comp.   Strange Tales from Many Lands.

SUMMARY: Eleven tales from different countries including "The Werewolf" from Spain, "The Inn that Wasn't There" from China, and "The Boy in the Secret Valley" from Iceland.

1. Tales. [1. Folklore] I. Lazarevich, Mila, illus. II. Title.

PZ8.1.L73St   398.2

ISBN 0-385-02167-4 Trade

0-385-09733-6 Prebound

Library of Congress Catalog Card Number 74–6668

BOOK DESIGN BY BENTE HAMANN

First Edition

FOR HAROLD, GLENN, AND JOHN

CONTENTS

vii

Contents

Contents

Strange Tales from Many Lands

To the Reader

It's MIDNIGHT and I'm alone in the study. Outside the snow is falling. It makes no sound as it falls, but still I seem to hear it. The wind pushes against the window and I shiver—not from the cold, but from the thought of it. The phone rings. I rush to answer it, but there's a sudden click at the other end. Was it a wrong number? Perhaps . . .

Everyone has had experiences that can't really be explained; they have a quality of wonder, magic, and mystery about them. A curtain moves, but there is no breeze. The doorbell rings, but no one is there. A room is familiar, but you've never seen it before. Your cat hisses, but nothing is in sight to make it angry or afraid.

Whether or not you believe in the supernatural, strange things do happen. They can be humorous, serious, wonderful, or eerie like the tales in this book that come from different lands. There's a piper who enters the cave of the Little People and is never seen again. There's an inn by the side of the road at night that vanishes at dawn. There's a doll that comes to life and a man who lives for centuries.

All these tales have some element of the inexplicable. They are strange tales—stranger than the ring of a bell when no one is at the door or the fluttering of a curtain when there is no breeze.

FREYA LITTLEDALE

1

THE
PIPER OF KEIL

Barbara Ker Wilson

I n Kintyre there is a great cave whose black mouth yawns wide among the cliffs of that rocky coast line. Long ago this cave was the home of the Little People. Men say that beyond its dark opening there are narrow, winding passages that stretch far inland; and somewhere in the midst of all these tortuous pathways was the great hall of the Little People, lit by a thousand fairy tapers, and echoing to the music of a thousand fairy minstrels. Here they would dance and hold their revels, and wait upon their Queen; and here, too, they would pronounce judgment on any mortal whom they found trespassing in their domain.

But few men dared to venture past the black entrance

of the great cave; for the people who dwelt along this western coast knew well the dangers and enchantments that might befall a mortal man who trespassed on fairy ground.

Now at Keil there lived a bold piper named Alasdair, whose playing was famed throughout Kintyre. He would often play his pipes when his neighbors gathered together after the day's work was done, setting their feet a-dancing. to the lilt of a reel, and playing the age-old airs that his forefathers had piped before him, while the foaming ale-stoup was passed round for good cheer and the peat-fire flame, rekindled with a blessing, cast its warm glow all about. And always there would be with Alasdair his little terrier dog, for the two of them were as fond of each other as a mother and her bairn or a good wife and her man.

On one such evening, when the merriment was at its height, Alasdair paused at the end of one of his fine tunes, and being well cheered by many a draught from the ale-stoup, he called out to the company, "Now I'll pipe ye a tune as good as any that's played by the wee folk themselves in the great cave yonder by the shore."

And he took up his pipes again and prepared to play. But there were many in the company who looked askance at his words, for it was a bold boast that the piper had made, and they all of them knew well that the wee folk were ever jealous of a mortal who strove to equal their abilities.

Before Alasdair could get more than a note or two out of his pipes, a certain farmer called Iain MacGraw spoke up and said, "Och, Alasdair, ye'd best take back the words ye have spoken. It's true enough that ye're the bravest piper in all Kintyre, but we all of us know that the wee folk who dwell in yonder great cave can play music far beyond our own imagining. It can aye charm a bairn from its mother's arms, or a man from his true love's side."

The piper smiled, and he answered proud and clear, "Ye've said your say, and I'll take up your words, Iain MacGraw. I'll wager ye that I can play my pipes right through the pathways of yon great cave this very night and come out again with no harm befallen me, for there'll be no fairy minstrel to challenge my way with sweeter music or a braver tune than this—"

And while the neighbors gasped among themselves at his foolhardy words, Alasdair lifted the pipes to his lips once more and broke into the skirling lilt of *The Nameless Tune*. And no one among that company had ever heard him play sweeter music or a braver air.

But Alasdair's daring boast had reached the knowledge of the Little Folk themselves, as they held revel in their great hall, and there was anger against the scornful piper of Keil. The thousand fairy minstrels pitched their immortal music on a wilder note, and the thousand fairy tapers flickered as the Elf Queen herself prepared a strong enchantment to fall upon the bold piper when he should enter her domain. It may be that a foreboding of this enchantment came to the piper's little dog, for the hairs stiffened along his back and he growled low in his throat as Alasdair stepped out from the neighbors' gathering and made his way to the cliffside, still playing *The Nameless Tune*. But the dog loved his master too well ever to desert him, and he followed close by his heels as Alasdair approached the black entrance of that great cave.

When they got there, his neighbors stood well aside as the piper strode unfaltering into the darkness, his kilt swinging to his step and his bonnet set jauntily on his head.

And by his heels went his faithful little dog. The neighbors strained their eyes to glimpse the last of him as he went away, and long after he had passed beyond their sight they heard the gay, clear music of his pipes. Then there was more than one among the company who shook his head and said, "I fear we'll never more see our brave piper of Keil."

It was not long before the gay piping stopped on a sudden with a dreadful squeal. And echoing, echoing through those twisting passageways until it reached the very mouth of that great cave came the noise of eldritch laughter. Then silence. And as the neighbors still stood there, trembling with fear for the fate of their bonny piper, there came limping out of the cave a poor, whimpering little beast with its eyeballs starting out of its head in fright. It had never a hair left on its body; and it was hard to recognize Alasdair's little terrier, who ran far from the cave as though the green fairy hounds themselves had been unleashed to chase him.

But there was no sign of Alasdair himself; and though some waited until long after dawn had come across the water, and though they called his name with their hands cupped to their mouths, the piper of Keil was never seen again. And there was not a man in all Kintyre who would venture through the black opening in the cliffside to seek him for they had every one heard that eerie laughter, which no man could remember without feeling a stroking of his spine.

But that is not quite the end of the story of the piper of Keil. One night as Iain MacGraw and his good wife were sitting by the fireside at their farm a few miles inland, the woman suddenly bent her ear to the hearthstone.

"Do you not hear the sound of pipes, good man?" she asked her husband.

The farmer listened in his turn, and at last he looked up and there was amazement in his eye. For the sound that they could hear was the playing of *The Nameless Tune*, and they knew full well that the piper was Alasdair himself, doomed by the Little Folk to wander forever through the maze of passageways that stretched far inland below the ground.

Then, as they listened, the sound of the tune died away and they heard the voice of the piper himself raised in this lament:

> *"I doubt, I doubt*
> *I'll never win out.*
> *Ochone! for my ageless sorrow."*

.   .   .   .   .

Today men say that still there are folk who have heard the far-away sound of the piper's playing at the place where Iain MacGraw's farm once stood; and always the tune is interspersed with that despairing cry.

THE INN
THAT WASN'T
THERE

Frederick H. Martens

ONCE upon a time there was a merchant who was traveling toward Shantung with his wares. As it grew dark, a heavy storm blew up from the north, and he chanced to see an inn at one side of the road. The merchant went in to get something to eat and order lodgings for the night, but the folk at the inn objected to the presence of this stranger among them. Yet a kindly old man took pity and said, "We have just prepared a meal for warriors who have come a long distance, and we have nothing left to serve you. But there is a little side room which is still free, and there you may stay overnight." With these words he led the merchant into it.

But the merchant could not sleep because of his hunger

and thirst. Outside he could hear the noise of men and horses. And since all these proceedings did not seem quite natural, he got up and opened the door very quietly. He saw the whole inn filled with soldiers eating and drinking and talking about battles of which he had never heard. Their uniforms resembled those he had seen on ancient scrolls.

Suddenly they called, "The general is coming!" and all the soldiers hurried out to greet him. Then the merchant saw a procession with many paper lanterns, and riding in their midst was a man of martial appearance with a long white beard. He entered the inn while the soldiers guarded the door and awaited his commands. Then the innkeeper served food and drink to which the general did full justice.

When he finished, his officers entered and he said to them, "You have now been under way for some time. Go back to your men. I shall rest a little myself. There will be time enough to beat the assembly when the order to advance is given."

The officers withdrew and the gates were locked for the night. Then the white-bearded general entered a room where the light of a lamp shone in the darkness. The merchant stole from his quarters and looked through a crack in the door.

Within the room was a bed of bamboo without covers or pillows. The lamp stood on the floor. The merchant watched in horror as the general took off his head and placed it on the bed. Then the light went out.

Overcome by terror, the merchant hurried back to his room as fast as he could. He lay down on the cot where he tossed about sleepless all night.

At last he heard a cock crow in the distance, and he

saw that dawn was stealing along the sky. He was shivering with cold. And when he looked about him, there he was lying in the middle of a thick clump of brush. Round about him was a wilderness—not a house, not even a grave was to be seen anywhere.

In spite of being chilled, the merchant ran about three miles till he reached an old farmhouse. The farmer opened the door and asked with astonishment where he came from at that early hour.

Then the merchant told him about his experiences at the inn. But the farmer only shook his head. "You must be mistaken," said he. "There is no inn within fifty miles from here. Though I have heard there was one once— hundreds of years ago. Soldiers used to stay there . . . led by a general with a long white beard."

TOKUTARO

Bernard Henderson and C. Calvert

MANY years ago, Kanaya, a maker of clogs, lived with his wife in the city of Nara. This man was known as an honest workman, and therefore had no lack of customers, so that he and his wife, Kiyu, might have lived in comfort, and very happily, but for one bitter sorrow. All their married life they had yearned for children, and had made many pilgrimages, especially to the shrines of Jizo, wearying the god with passionate prayers for a family.

But none had been granted them. And now that they were old, when work was over for the day, they would sit in silence round the warmth of the *hibachi*, not so much because the air was chill, but because of the coldness within their hearts.

One evening the clog maker, having closed the shop, sat down in the inner room to wait for his wife. She had gone out that afternoon, in spite of a heavy rain storm and, returning at dusk, had hastily left again. Kanaya was surprised and anxious at her long absence. Lately he had noticed a strangeness in Kiyu's manner; she had also been away from home during a part of every morning, and often in the afternoon as well.

He was relieved, therefore, when he heard her come in. She lingered a few moments in the shop and then, entering the room, silently began to prepare their evening meal. It seemed to Kanaya that her eyes sparkled, and that she moved with an odd, joyous lightness.

When the meal was over and the table cleared, Kiyu sat down beside Kanaya and, laying her hand on his, said, "Honorable husband, I have today done a very foolish thing for which, no doubt, our neighbors would think me mad. But you, I feel sure, will understand."

She rose eagerly, went out into the shop, and returned, bearing in her arms a large parcel wrapped in fine rice paper.

Sitting down, she laid it tenderly on her knees, removed the covering, and showed her astonished husband a boy doll of unusual size and workmanship. "This doll is called Tokutaro," said she.

It was a fantastic figure, large as a child of three years. The face was beautiful and perfectly modeled, the locks and eyelashes were of real hair, the feet and hands so carefully fashioned that they seemed those of a living child, and the clothes were of the richest flowered silk. So lifelike was the doll that the old man held his breath.

After a while he reached out timidly and felt Tokutaro's face, then the hands and feet, on which his wife pointed out the small, rosy nails, weeping for joy as she did so. Tears came into Kanaya's eyes.

"Truly," he said, "never till now have I understood 'The Sadness of Might Have Been!' But the will of the gods must be done! And now, tell me, how did you light on this rare wonder?"

Kiyu, resting her head on his shoulder, answered, "Did I not know you would understand! It may be that I am mistaken, but I think Jizo has at last taken pity on our loneliness. This is my tale.

"A week ago, in the shop of our neighbor, Teoyo, among the vases, armor, cabinets, and other old and choice things in which he deals, I saw the doll, and my heart leaped out to it. I looked long, and then walked away with difficulty, for it seemed to me that its eyes were fixed eagerly on mine. That look haunted me day and night. I said to myself that it was a foolish fancy, born of the yearning of a childless woman, but I could not master my longing. Every day, in the morning and in the afternoon, I stood outside the shop, trembling lest Tokutaro should be sold.

"On the fourth day, desperate with desire, I went in and enquired the price. Teoyo demanded twenty *ryos*, and I did not try to bargain, knowing that he is a stubborn man. Very unwillingly I went away, for I could not think of wasting so much of your hard-earned money on a whim. But, the next day I returned, and the following day also, morning and evening.

"This afternoon, as I stood outside the shop in the driving rain that had cleared the street, Teoyo suddenly called me. His voice was very gentle and strange.

"'Neighbor,' he said, 'very surely your heart is set on this doll, for not the gods themselves could lure anyone to such faithful pilgrimages as you have made here these seven days. It is plain that some deity is concerned in this; but you shall judge. Every morning I have found Tokutaro's cheeks so stained with weeping that I have found it difficult to clear away the traces. Nor is this all. Last night Jizo appeared to me in a dream, commanding me to let you have the doll. Take it, therefore, and give me what you will, or even nothing at all, for it is not well to bargain with the gods.'

"But I, my husband, did not think it right to take advantage of his compassion, and refused the gift except at a fair price. Thereupon he told me that he had paid five *ryos* for the doll. This sum he would gladly take, but nothing more, on condition that I did not mention the matter to anyone. So I hastened home for the money, and when the business was settled, I remember how Tokutaro seemed to smile at me.

"I feel sure that the doll once belonged to some great family and was much loved. Many a little one must have fondled him, and so given him life, for I feel that in some way Tokutaro is more than wood and plaster. Have we not often heard how these figures acquire a soul if they are tenderly loved?"

"Honorable wife," Kanaya answered, "you have done wisely and well. Already it seems to me that our house is less empty. Tokutaro shall not want for love, even though it is an old and withered one. We will, however, keep this matter a secret between us. I fear the jests of our neighbors."

On the morrow they contrived a hiding place for Tokutaro, out of which, when they were alone, they would take him and feast their eyes on his beauty. Kiyu was never weary of fondling him. And when the old couple sat down to their meals, they would laughingly offer him food.

Indeed, before long they began to regard Tokutaro as a living child—their own flesh and blood. Many a time, while busy at the household work, Kiyu sang the words of a poet:

> "*As flowers seem sweetest, when they pierce*
> *The barren winter snow,*
> *Dear Blossom of my withered age,*
> *Lovely art thou, aglow*
> *With beauty, like dream children seen*
> *Through the slow, silent rain*
> *Of tears with which I craved for thee*
> *So long, my son, in vain!*"

In spite of all their caution, news of these doings spread, but, far from deriding the childless couple, neighbors spoke reverently of their seeming folly, so that after a while the old people did not hide the matter. Children took to haunting the house in order to play with Tokutaro, and the place was full of young laughter and voices, to the joy of Kanaya and his wife.

Their pleasure in the figure increased daily. When the weather was cold they would lay Tokutaro, wrapped in warm clothing, between them in the bed, and fall asleep, happier for such company.

But they were to experience yet greater joys, for gradually they became aware of strange happenings.

At night it often seemed to them that a tiny hand was fondling their faces, and that a frail form was nestling close to them for warmth. Yet, when roused by the touch, nothing stirred, and wistfully, they fell asleep again. So great was their yearning that neither spoke of these experiences, but each was aware that the other knew.

One winter night Kanaya, wakened by gentle fingers that seemed unusually insistent, heard a stealthy sound.

Someone was stirring in the shop!

Before he could rise the shoji were withdrawn, and he saw two robbers enter with swords. Threatening violence, they demanded money.

Roused by their voices, Kiyu sat up and gave a cry, not of fear but of wonder, for she beheld Tokutaro standing before the men. Their eyes, glazed by terror, were fixed on the doll. The figure raised its right arm and waved away the robbers who fled in panic from the shop.

Kanaya lit the lantern and saw his wife kneeling before Tokutaro, who was lying once more on the bed. His eyes and smile were those of a living child.

There was no more sleep for the old people that night; till dawn they knelt side by side, speaking in whispers about their son.

Some weeks after, about midnight, Kiyu was awakened by light anxious fingers on her cheek. Looking up, she hastily roused her husband, for a steady roar of fire filled the air. By the shoji that closed the entrance into the shop stood Tokutaro, beckoning to them.

They snatched up a few valuables, took their little hoard of money from its hiding place, together with the image of Jizo, and followed Tokutaro out into the street. It was empty of people, but filled with the flickering lights and shadows of fire. Flames were gushing out of their neighbor's house which, the next moment, flared like a torch. A red wave leaped out, washed over their own dwelling, and swept up toward the stars in a fountain of crimson fire.

Tokutaro led them across the road, where he stopped, leaning motionless against the wall. The old woman caught him up in her arms, while Kanaya hastened to help his neighbors who were pouring out into the red-lit street.

By this time their own house had become a roaring furnace, fed by the wooden soles of the clogs stacked in the shop. Had they delayed but a few moments, they would have perished.

Many months later, when Kanaya and his wife had rebuilt their house, they set up a special altar to Jizo, and before it, in a lacquer cabinet, Tokutaro had a place of honor; for after the fire, awe mingled with the old people's love.

Some years after, Kanaya died; and for months the forlorn wife, gazing into Tokutaro's eyes, saw them filled with tears and sorrow, answering hers.

She sold the shop and withdrew to a small country house. There she lived with Tokutaro, blessing the mercy of the gods who had so comforted her old age.

It was her delight to clothe Tokutaro in robes of costly silk. Hour upon hour she sat looking upon him, glorious as a butterfly. Moreover, unlike mortal children, his beauty was untouched by time.

One thought troubled Kiyu: what would become of her treasure after she was dead? Surely the gods, whose instrument he had been, would provide! Nevertheless, to make the future more certain, she went to the priests of the Temple of Jizo and entrusted Tokutaro to their keeping after she had gone from this world.

Two years later neighbors found Kiyu dead, holding Tokutaro in her arms. But when the priests from the Temple of Jizo arrived to claim the wonderful doll, Tokutaro could not be found, nor was he ever again seen familiarly among men.

Mourners, however, returning home from the graveyard on the first day of the Festival of the Dead, declared they had beheld Tokutaro making offerings, burning incense, and pouring water over the tombstones of Kanaya and his wife.

THE WATER-BULL

Dora Broome

ONCE there was a farmer called Ewan Kerruish who was the most bad-tempered person on the Isle of Man. Nobody would work for him except his wife, Elsby, and Illiam Corkish, an old farm hand. If it hadn't been for those two, who slaved night and day, the land would have gone to ruin. Never a word of thanks did they get, but only, "Do this, woman," or "Is it drink that's in you, Illiam, or are you sleeping?" So cross and rude was Ewan that none of the neighbors would come near him except on business. And his wife, Elsby, who had been the prettiest girl in the parish before she was married, grew thin and pale.

One evening, when Ewan was walking by the river, what should he see, feeding amongst his cattle, but a Tarroo-Ushtey, one of the water-bulls who live in rivers and deep pools. A fine-looking beast he was, with shining coat, and if Ewan hadn't seen his short sharp ears and evil eyes, he wouldn't have known him for a fairy creature at all.

"What do you mean by eating the good sweet grass that's meant for your betters!" cried Ewan. And he hit the water-bull across the back with his stick.

The beast threw up his head and gave Ewan one look out of those wicked eyes of his, and then away he went to the river. He dove beneath the water and Ewan saw him no more.

Ewan drove his cows home, and when he told his wife about the water-bull, she was very annoyed.

"Why couldn't you leave the beast be?" she asked. " 'Tis not a bite of sweet grass you'd be missing. I wouldn't wonder but there'll be an evil spell upon us with a blight on the crops now."

"Hold your tongue, woman," said Ewan. "Let that wicked one try any of his capers on me, and he'll see who's master here."

Elsby left out a cup of milk for the Little People every night, but for all that, when the corn came up, sure enough, there was a blight on it.

" 'Tis old Teare, the Fairy Doctor, we're needing to put a charm on the place," said Elsby. " 'Tis the only way to break the spell."

"Fairy my heels!" shouted Ewan. "I'm not throwing good money after bad. Let that creature come to my fields again and I'll break the horns on him."

"Them that pokes the fire with a short stick is like to get burned," said Elsby. But say what she would, she couldn't put any sense into Ewan.

"I'll teach the beast to keep clear of my fields," said he.

The next evening he set off for the river with a long rope over his arm. When he saw the water-bull, he crept up behind and, throwing the rope over his horns, drew the knot tight. Up went the creature's heels, and down went his head, and he bellowed like a foghorn.

"I have you now, safe enough, you old devil," said Ewan, but he spoke too soon. With a mighty pull, the rope was twitched out of Ewan's hands, and away went the bull into the river with the spray flying and the rope trailing after him.

What a temper Ewan went home in! He rampaged up and down so that Elsby didn't even dare leave a cup of milk or a crumb of cheese for the Little People.

Sure enough, when the potatoes came up, there was a blight on them too. Black scabs, as big as two fingers were on them.

"If you won't seek the Fairy Doctor, then I must," insisted Elsby. "I'm thinking hard of the farm being ruined for want of a bit of sense."

"Where there's a woman there's no end to trouble," grumbled Ewan, but at last he went to see old Teare, the Fairy Doctor.

Old Teare heard his story to the end. Then he said, "There's witchcraft in it, for certain. . . . A terrible uncivil man you are, and always have been, and I'd advise you to be mending your ways. Go home now and make a little stick from a branch of the rowan tree. The next time you see the Tarroo-Ushtey, stroke him with the peeled stick and speak kindly to him."

"Speak kindly to that evil one!" exclaimed Ewan. "Why I thought you'd be giving me a thousand curses to put on him. You can whistle to the birds, for I'm told you understand the way they speak, but don't be telling me to speak kindly to the Tarroo-Ushtey."

And away he went in a towering rage.

Although he had been so unpleasant to old Teare, he didn't forget about the stick. He cut a switch of rowan, peeled it, and off he went in the evening, with the stick in his hand.

The water-bull was feeding amongst the cattle in the peaceful evening light. When he saw Ewan coming, he lifted his head and gave another of those wicked looks from his little eyes. Ewan crept up very quietly, with his hand behind his back, and when he got quite close, he touched the beast on the back with the switch. The bull stood still, trembling, for he couldn't do anything against the power of the rowan stick.

"That's got you, my brave boy," said Ewan. And he gave the creature another scutch and led him home. Elsby was frightened when she saw them coming.

"You're not going to stable that one with the cattle!" she cried. "Look at the wicked eyes on him! Let go of the rope so he can go back to the river."

"'Tis to the market I'm taking him, woman," said Ewan, "and selling him for good money. Who's to know what he is unless I tell them?"

"Selling him!" exclaimed Elsby. "Why 'tis clean mad you are. Who would buy him with that wicked look of his? You'll find yourself at the bottom of the river if you meddle with the Tarroo-Ushtey."

"Hold your peace, woman," Ewan told her. "If you keep your mouth shut, we'll get a good price for him."

He led the water-bull into the stable and tied him up for the night. Next morning he set off, and the beast walked along quiet as a lamb, though every now and then he looked at Ewan from the corner of his eye.

There were many farmers at the market, and some spoke to Ewan, but although the water-bull stood still, his sleek coat shining in the sun, no person asked the price of him.

At last, just before sunset, Tommy-Dick of Ballachrink came along. Tommy wasn't so clever as most people, but for all that, he was good to his old mother.

"That's a fine beast you have there," said Tommy. "Is he quiet and steady?"

"You can see for yourself," answered Ewan, and he touched the water-bull with the stick of rowan.

"There's a queer look in his eye," said Tommy-Dick. "I wouldn't say but he'd be jumping to the moon one night."

"Jumping my heels," replied Ewan. "I'm wanting to get home now, so you can have him for the price I gave for him."

"I wouldn't like him to be kicking up a randyboose at home," said Tommy.

"You only have to stroke him with this little stick and he'll be quiet," Ewan answered. Then he smiled to himself, thinking that Tommy wouldn't drive the creature far before he'd be off to the river.

"If you'll get on his back and ride him to the end of the road, I'll take him," said Tommy-Dick, "for if you can ride a bull to market, you can take him home by the nose."

"That's a bargain," agreed Ewan. And he got on the Tarroo-Ushtey's back, gave him a little scutch with the stick, and off they went. But they hadn't gone far when somehow the little stick slipped from his hand and fell on the road. Ewan tried to lean over and pick it up, but the beast was too quick for him. Down went his head, and off with him, thundering down the road as if the Evil One himself was after them.

The people in the town scattered to right and left as the bull came charging down. "Mad bull! Mad bull!" they shouted. Some urged that he should be shot, while others cried that it would kill the man too. Away they went, with Ewan holding on for dear life, and when Ewan saw the beast was heading for the river, he was in a sweat of fear.

"I'm thinking Elsby'll be a widow before night," said he. And he began to wish he'd been kinder to her. "I'd ask her pardon," he thought, "if I could see her again before I'm drowned."

They came in sight of the farm, and there was Elsby, looking up and down the road to see if her husband was coming. On went the water-bull, with Ewan clinging to him.

"What in the world are you doing, Ewan?" cried Elsby.

Ewan was just going to say something uncivil, when he remembered it might be the last word he'd ever speak to her.

" 'Tis the handsomest woman you are in the parish," he called. And with that, away down the road they went while Elsby stared after them.

The beast headed straight for the river, but just as he was about to plunge in, Ewan gave one mighty jump and rolled off into the shallow water near the bank.

The next minute he heard a terrible bellow, and down went the beast into the deep river.

Ewan crawled out of the water on his hands and knees,

picked himself up, and never stopped running until he reached home. And wasn't Elsby glad to see him, even though he had been a bad-tempered husband.

"Elsby," said he, when he had dry clothes and had eaten and rested, "you'd better be leaving a cup of milk for the Little People tonight, and a bit of fire to warm them too. A civil word will hurt none."

And from that time on, there wasn't a better-tempered man on the Island than Ewan Kerruish.

THE
MYSTERIOUS
FIG TREE

Charles Godfrey Leland

O N the Via del Fico in Florence there was once an ancient palace with a magnificent garden. In the garden was a fig tree which was said to have grown of itself—without ever having been planted.

The owner of the palace was a rich and powerful lord. He was proud of the tree's beauty, but its mysteries disturbed him. Although many people had tried to cut off boughs from the tree, the next day they were replaced by a perfect new growth with fully ripe fruit. And it was not the least marvel of the tree that it was always in full bloom with an abundance of ripe figs—even in winter when snow was on the ground. But there was something strange about the figs; they were never to be enjoyed.

Once a visitor to the palace could not resist the fruit. As she reached her arm to pluck a fig, the ground quivered beneath her. Then she heard an unearthly howl, and a great black dog appeared at her side. The beast seized the woman's skirt between his teeth and pulled her away from the tree. Then its howling ceased, and the dog seemed to disappear in the earth below.

On another occasion, when the lord gave a splendid ball at the palace, one of his guests plucked a fig from the tree and ate it. The man felt sharp pains in his chest and went to his room. As he lay down, a girl clad in white suddenly entered and began to whirl round and round, making loud buzzing sounds as she moved. And when she perceived the look of horror on the man's face, she smiled and vanished from the room. The man soon recovered, but never again did he go near the fig tree.

One day the gardener was digging near the tree when he found a tablet of stone. He ran to the lord and showed him the words inscribed on it:

> *Respect the tree, and let it be,*
> *From branch to root, nor touch its fruit!*
> *Of itself the tree did grow,*
> *From a dog who long ago,*
> *Enchanted by the fairies' power,*
> *Was buried here in mystic hour.*
> *Therefore we bid you let it stand,*
> *And if you follow the command*
> *You will be happy all your days.*
> *But woe to him who disobeys!*

But the lord had no faith in old legends, nor love for such mysteries as these. "It is time to put an end to all this superstition," said he. "A great black dog, a girl spinning round and round, and now this tablet—I've had enough!

I am determined to see whether all my prosperity depends on a mere fig tree. Go at once and cut it down. Then tear it up, roots and branches—completely!"

The gardener was terrified, but he could not disobey the lord's wishes. So he went back to the garden and began to dig up the tree. But the moment his shovel touched the ground, he heard great wailing sounds in the earth. At once he threw down the shovel and ran back to the palace. "I dare not destroy it!" said he. "There are voices in the earth. Do come and listen for yourself."

But the lord only answered, "Away with your superstitions. This time we will see whether the tree will grow again. Destroy it!"

And so it was done. The tree did not grow again. It passed away forever . . . and with it the health and prosperity of the lord. For he lost all his wealth and died soon after from an illness that no one could name.

TIGER WOMAN

Eleanore M. Jewett

N IM SAN had a large family of boys and girls, but no wife. Since her death they had all lived with his mother, a gentle old lady who spoiled the children and could never say no to their desires. They had brass-studded chests filled with strings of money, each coin with a hole in its center so that a large number could be strung on a single cord. All Korean households kept their money in strings, and Nim San was fortunate in the length and number that he had stored away. He was a rich man. But there comes an end to all good material possessions if they are not replenished, and there came a time when the last string had been taken out of the last chest and there soon would not be a single coin left.

Nim San was dismayed, but not the children. They had always had everything they wanted and had never stopped to consider how or where their father had got it.

"Please, Honorable Parent," said one of the boys, "I shall need a new padded coat for the winter. Mine is much too short in the sleeves."

"We shall all need new coats for the New Year festival," cried the other boys.

"And new straw sandals, and wooden-soled boots for the rainy season—and soft shoes, too, with the toes turning up."

"And we need another kang-jar for kimchee—there are so many of us," the grandmother put in.

"And lots and lots of silk string and colored paper for our new kites," said the littlest boy.

"Honorable Father," one of the girls managed to put her word in. "I am old enough for a jeweled comb and all of us need new ribbons." A chorus of "ye', ye'" came from all the little girls who had gathered around him. "We want— We want—"

"There are sweetmeats in Seoul better than our home-made ones—"

"Will you buy us—"

"Father, we need—"

Nim San threw up his hands in despair. "But, my children, there is no more money left!"

Silence followed for a few moments, then the chatter broke out again. "But, Honorable Father, we must have—" And so it went, more demanding than ever. Apparently nobody, not even Grandmother, could understand that without money there could be no more buying. Nim San tried to explain but at last gave it up and fled from the house, unable to bear the situation longer.

Not far from his home the mountains began. Their green wooded sides were showing patches of gold and scarlet, russet and purple, for the autumn frosts were already tingling in the air, but Nim San had no eyes for the beauty around him. His heart was so heavy that he thought he might better die.

He climbed up and up, scarcely noticing where he was going, and when at last he roused himself from his sad thoughts and looked around, he realized that he was in a part of the country quite strange to him. He was not exactly lost, for the trail he had absent-mindedly followed was definite and wound on around the side of the hill and undoubtedly would lead him somewhere. Near him he noticed a small grass-roofed hut close to the steep mountain, and as he felt suddenly very weary, he walked over to it, pushed the bamboo door open and stepped inside. A light snow had begun to fall and he felt chilled to the very marrow of his bones. There being, of course, no heat inside the hut, it seemed damp and colder than outside, so he left the door open, sitting on the floor beside the high sill.

Before long he was astonished to see, coming up the trail toward him, a very beautiful sedan chair richly fitted out with silken hangings and borne by four runners in handsome livery. They came close to the hut and then paused, the bearers breathing heavily after their hard climb. Behind them at some distance an elderly woman in the customary dress of a servant followed, moving slowly and with difficulty, almost at the end of her strength.

37

The curtains of the chair parted and a woman looked out. Upon seeing Nim San she withdrew again in confusion, for it is not proper for a woman to be seen by any strange man, much less to converse with him. But after a moment she looked out again, motioned her bearers to set down the chair and stepped out. She paid no attention to Nim San but ran back to the old woman, put a supporting arm about her and led her to the hut. Nim San, bowing courteously, moved aside and helped settle the exhausted servant on the floor. Impulsively he took his own padded coat off and laid it over her, for she was shivering in spite of her layers of cotton clothing.

Then Nim San and the lady from the sedan chair looked at each other. Never had he seen so beautiful or so unusual a face; young, with skin like palely tinted ivory, red lips and delicate pointed chin, hair as black as midnight, and thin black eyebrows. From under these her narrow slanted eyes stared out at him—green like those of a cat. Noticing his astonishment, the lady smiled faintly, and Nim San was covered with confusion at his own rudeness.

"Honorable Lady," said he, bowing very low, "I ask a thousand pardons. I—I—is there not something I can do for you or for your woman? The snow is falling more heavily now and already the evening chill has sharpened the air—" He paused, scarcely knowing how to meet the unblinking keenness of those green eyes.

"Thank you, good Sir." The lady's voice was silken soft, unlike any he had ever heard. "You have already shown a remarkably unselfish kindness in placing your own coat over my old nurse, but now you must put it on again before you are chilled through."

She clapped her hands and the bearers of the sedan came forward. Following her commands, they carried the old woman to the chair, laid her within it, and handed Nim San his coat again.

"And now," continued the lady, "I bid you follow after me. My house lies not many miles distant, in the heart of a hidden valley. There you will be welcome as my guest and can pass the night in warmth and comfort, and continue your journey in the morning." She climbed again into the sedan chair and drew the curtains. The runners picked up the poles and started at a jog trot, taking the trail farther into the mountains.

Nim San followed them. He had some difficulty in keeping their pace and soon fell behind, but in time he rounded a beetling bluff and came upon a narrow road leading straight down into a deep valley.

The snow had ceased falling and the air was tangy with the scent of evergreens. The sun came out and it seemed warmer as he descended. Then the pines and hemlocks gave place to trees whose flaming scarlet and gold vied with the sunset splendor of the western sky.

A large and beautiful palace stood directly in front of him, almost as fine and extensive as the emperor's own. Servants met him and took him to the men's apartment, where he bathed and put on the rich white silk apparel which they laid out for him. Then on a gold and lacquer tray his dinner was brought to him, served in shining brass bowls—rice and beans, fowl and kimchee and many special delicacies, all of the best and tastiest. He sat on his heels on the floor in front of the tray and, finding himself very hungry, made a good meal of it.

After the empty bowls and the spoons and chopsticks

had been removed and he had washed his fingers in scented water, he was taken to the inner court, where he found the lady waiting to receive him. The old woman had evidently recovered for she sat crouched in a corner of the room, as motionless as a statue.

They had a pleasant evening together. The lady was gracious and friendly. She soon put him at his ease and he found himself telling of his motherless children, their continual but entirely understandable demands and his despair at being now unable to supply them.

The lady bade him lay aside his cares. "I live in this big house alone but for my old nurse and the other servants," she said. "There is no end to my wealth and my possessions, and most gladly will I give you all that you desire. Tomorrow morning my servants will load a donkey for you with presents for your honorable mother and for the children, and strings of money for you to use as you have need. Only be my friend and come again to my palace when the winter evenings are long and cold. We will play at changki [chess] together and while away the long hours sitting here upon the warm floor. And always when you come I will supply all your needs for your home and family."

Nim San could do nothing but bow over and over again, murmuring his thanks while tears of relief and gratitude ran down his cheeks.

The next morning he found a donkey laden with the gifts from the lady standing in the courtyard. Servants stood about ready to serve him, but he saw no sign of their mistress and at last left his good-bys and repeated thanks with the head man who promised to deliver them, and started on the long journey home.

The surprise and delight of his old mother and still more of his children can well be imagined, and for a long time there were no demands from them. Nim San lived happily enough in the midst of his contented family, with money to spare and all their needs and desires satisfied. He thought often of the strange beautiful lady with the green eyes and her rich palace on the other side of the mountains and at length decided to visit her again as he had agreed to do.

He had no trouble in finding his way though it was a long and difficult climb and bitter cold now that winter had set in. The lady seemed more lovely and charming than ever, and after that, all through the winter, he visited her again and yet again. Often she loaded him with gifts, but not always. Sometimes they would just spend a contented evening together playing chess or talking. He would sleep on a thick mat on the warm comfortable floor in the men's apartment and then go home the next morning without seeing her again and with no gifts or messages from her. He began to prefer not to be always indebted to her, for he realized that he loved her and wanted to make her his wife. The rich gifts he was constantly receiving from her, while he gave her nothing in return, made things awkward. Indeed, the whole situation was awkward. There seemed to be no one who could act as a go-between for her, as is customary in all Korean marriages. Always the old nurse sat on her heels, motionless as a stone image, in the room with them, but there appeared to be no relative or proper person to whom his mother could go and discuss marriage for him.

Nim San was thinking about these things one day in early spring as he climbed the steep trail over the moun-

41

tain. Suddenly he saw a strange white cloud rolling down upon him. It seemed like a huge soft ball so distinct and round that he expected to feel the impact of it as it fell upon him. He did not, however. It quietly surrounded him, shutting out instantly all sight of the valley beneath him and the tops of the hills above him and even the newly budding trees and bushes all around him. Mist, gray, thick, damp, cold, closed him in so completely that he stopped where he was, not daring to take a step forward or back.

Suddenly from somewhere above his head he heard a harsh voice saying, "Get down upon the ground, Nim San. Make reverent obeisance to the soul of your ancestor."

Nim San, trembling with terror, fell upon his knees, covering his eyes with his hands. "What would you, Great and Honorable Sir?" he said, touching his head to the earth nine times.

"I have come from the world beyond the farthest mountains to warn you," the voice continued. "Listen carefully to what I say and obey me."

There was a long moment of silence. Nim San, though still shaking with fear and astonishment, dropped his hands and looked about him. He could see nothing but the blank gray wall of mist. "Speak further, Honorable Ancestor," said he tremblingly. "Your humble and dutiful descendant is listening."

"The woman you are bent upon visiting"—the voice was harsher than ever—"is no ordinary mortal, but a tiger. Did you not note the green eyes of her? Tiger-woman she is in very truth, permitted only for certain hours to take upon herself the form of a human."

Nim San gasped and then groaned. He had not realized the strength of his love for the lady, but now the thought of losing her, of her being other than she seemed, cut his heart deeply and miserably.

"Waste no time in foolish sorrow," the voice went on in a cold, pitiless tone. "Go at once to the palace as you intended. Do not wait for the servants to admit you but thrust open the bamboo door of the inner court *without knocking*. Then you will see the lady of your love in her true and terrible state. What is more important, if you catch her in the act of changing herself into human form she will have to continue a beast, a fierce and hated tiger, forever."

With that the mist folded back like a blanket, rolled down the mountainside and disappeared. The sun shone again over the hilltops for a few moments, then dropped behind them, for the late afternoon was wearing on. The trail showed clearly with the rough underbrush crowding it, and the valley in the distance grew soft in the lovely shades of the early spring twilight.

For a few moments Nim San was too shocked and bewildered to move. Then he got to his feet and, without allowing himself time to think, hurried on. He reached the palace just as the half light was darkening into night, rushed through the outer court to the bamboo door of the women's apartment. He was about to thrust it open without knocking, as he had been bidden to do, when something stayed his hand. Though the green-eyed lady might indeed be a terrible tiger, able by some magic art to appear human and deceive him, he could not take a mean advantage over her. Many a time her strange eyes had looked into his with kindness, friendliness and even love. She had been good to him and to his children. He could not find it in his heart thus to betray her.

His hand dropped and he was about to turn away from the bamboo door when it slowly opened. The old nurse stood there and silently motioned him to come in. Then she left him and for some time he remained alone, standing with his hands in his sleeves, his head bowed, wondering.

She entered again, noiselessly. Nim San did not hear or see her come. But suddenly the lady appeared with her. She stood in front of him, more beautiful and gracious than ever, tall, slim, in rich silken garments white as snow. Fearfully he looked into her face and cried out in his astonishment. Her eyes were no longer green but black and sparkling with joy and affection and—yes—amusement!

"Do not look so dumfounded, dear friend," said she, laughing. "All is as it should be! Come!" She led the way into the inner court and bade him sit beside her on the warm floor.

"You have this day saved me from a thousand years of grief and torment," she said. "In the spirit world I was condemned, for a sin I had committed, to take the form of a tiger for many generations. But every once in so often, for certain hours and certain days, it was permitted me to change into human form. If during my time as a woman I could win the love of a good man who, in spite of knowing my other state, would marry me, then I was to be allowed to stay human. There was one condition, however: neither he nor anyone must ever see me in the act of changing from tiger to woman or woman to tiger. If any mortal eyes should behold that great, mysterious act of magic, which none but the spirits that dwell beyond the farthest mountains know about or understand, then I would be condemned to keep my tiger shape unchanged for a thousand years, perhaps forever."

"So the soul of my ancestor spoke the truth," Nim San murmured, "but not the whole truth, and I would rather have you as my wife, whatever shape or form you held in some past life, than any woman in this world or that Other."

The lady's black almond eyes grew soft and tears welled up in them. "You see," she said, brushing away the bright drops, "this proves I am altogether human for neither beasts nor spirits, good or bad, can shed tears as humans do."

"But why should the soul of my ancestor counsel me to a deed of discourtesy and unkindness that would result only in sorrow to both of us?" Nim San was still puzzled.

"That was not the soul of your ancestor!" declared the lady. "It was an evil spirit that has long pursued me to destroy me, body and soul, forever! But now he can have no further power over me."

"Why is that?" asked Nim San, wondering.

"Because love is stronger than any evil," said the lady.

Now the rest of the story is easily guessed. Nim San married the lovely lady and took his children and his mother to the beautiful palace on the other side of the mountain. There they lived in great happiness together for the rest of their days.

THE SHEPHERD'S CHOICE

Helene Adeline Guerber

LONG ago a shepherd named Res tended his cattle high on an alp in Switzerland. Every evening, after the cattle were duly cared for, Res took the huge funnel through which he poured milk, and, reversing it, stepped out on the ledge of a rock and called to his sweetheart on the Seealp. Only the echo of her voice could be heard in answer to his call. When it grew dark, Res returned to his hut. There, he climbed up into the loft, lay down on his pallet and slept soundly until the next day.

Late one night Res was suddenly awakened by a crackling sound. He peered down from the loft and was startled by the sight of three strange men. He wanted to speak, but the odd appearance of the visitors kept him quiet.

47

Their faces were white—almost glowing. Their movements were slow and careful as if they were unaccustomed to moving their arms and legs.

The strangers seated themselves around a fire which they had kindled on his hearth. The largest of the three men kept stirring milk in his giant kettle. The next one brought more milk to add to it, while the third kept up a bright blaze by adding fuel to the fire from time to time.

Res watched the big man pour a red fluid into the kettle. Then the second man stepped to the door and, taking a huge horn, began to play a haunting melody. Low at first, it gradually roused the echoes and had a magical effect, for all the cattle came running up to him. They stood around in a circle as if to listen. When the musical performance ended, the tallest man poured the contents of the kettle into three vessels, and Res noted with surprise that the liquid in each one was a different color.

Just then the man looked up and pointed directly at Res. "Come down, shepherd," said he, "and drink from any bowl you please. If you drink the red liquid, you could be as strong as a giant and receive one hundred sheep. If you taste the green, you may have a large fortune. But if you choose the white, you may receive the alphorn and be able to play the haunting tune that charms cattle as well as men."

Frightened though he was, Res climbed down from the loft. He had been so enraptured by the music that its spell was still upon him. Without hesitation, he took a deep draught of the bowl containing the white liquid. When he set it down, the horn player congratulated him on his choice. "If you had drunk from either of the other bowls," said he, "you would surely have died, and centuries would have passed before the alphorn could have been offered to mankind again."

With these words, the unearthly visitors vanished from the hut. Only one trace of their presence remained—the alphorn!

Then, as the first gleams of light appeared in the east, Res put the horn to his lips. To his delight he found he could play as well as the mysterious stranger. And so he played to his sweetheart on the distant alp each summer's eve.

In the autumn they were married, and later their descendants inherited the amazing alphorn. More were made, exactly like the first, and generation after generation were charmed by its beauty. And thus the strange and wonderful music can be heard in the Alps of Switzerland to this very day.

THE WEREWOLF

S. G. C. Middlemore

ROSITA lived in that part of Spain where forests abound, and where the road to the nearest market town lay through those deep dark glades without a hut or a hovel anywhere near. She was the youngest of six children, and when her brothers and sisters went to Madrid and started life for themselves, a great deal of work fell upon her shoulders. Besides helping her mother with the cooking and cleaning, she had the cattle to pasture, the fowl to feed, the fish to catch, and the cotton and wool to spin and sell in the market town.

At one time Rosita's father was away from home on business. He had to sell some cattle and was obliged to go a long way off before he could get the price that he asked. And so it happened that during his absence, the supplies ran short. At length the meal and flour barrels were almost empty, and Rosita hardly knew what to do.

The winter was an unusually severe one, and the weather was bitterly cold. Her mother was just recovering from a long illness, and Rosita didn't want to leave her alone. Yet there was so little to eat that a journey to the market seemed inevitable. Rosita put it off from day to day, catching as many fish as she could in the nearest river. At last, however, everything came to an end. The meal and flour barrels were completely empty, and the river was frozen so hard that it was impossible to catch any fish.

One morning, therefore, Rosita started off to the nearest town which was five miles away. She was warmly dressed and carried her basket filled with spun thread to sell at the market. It took hours to make her way through the snowdrifts, and it was late before she could turn homeward again.

Rosita had been lucky with her marketing. She had sold the thread for quite a large sum, and with her basket full of the most necessary things, and with the barrels of meal and flour promised in a couple of days, she trudged along the snow tracks as happy as a queen.

It was dark when Rosita was still a couple of miles from home, so she lit her lantern and went on her way without thought of fear. Soon she met an old man who hobbled along with the aid of an old walking stick. He wore a battered felt hat and was wrapped in a torn brown cloak huddled up to the chin.

"Please," he said, "can you give me something to eat? I haven't had a bite of food all day."

The old man looked so starved, so poor, and so

wretched, that Rosita broke off a piece of bread from the loaf in her basket and gave it to him. He thanked her and ate it hungrily. But she noticed, while he ate his bread, that his teeth were sharp and pointed; and as the darkness deepened, his eyes had a queer long shape and seemed to turn green and narrow. But he spoke so pleasantly as they walked along together that Rosita thought no more of that queer look.

When they reached her home she said, "Poor man, you seem very weak and ill, and it is bitterly cold. I am sure my mother will give you food and shelter for tonight, and you can continue your journey in the morning."

"I shall be very grateful to you both," he replied.

Yet, for the first time in her life, Rosita was frightened. Her dog, Moro, who came bounding to meet her, suddenly turned cowering away; he howled as loud as he could while he crouched close to the wall near his kennel. And as the old man passed the sheepfolds and pigpens, the animals all ran to the farthest corners, while the hens tumbled over each other in fear, and lay on the floor in the remotest part of the roost.

And as soon as they got into the house, the little kitten began to spit, humped up her back, waved her tail, and disappeared under the bed. Rosita thought all this was very strange, but she said nothing. She only wished that she had not asked this old man to pass the night under their roof.

"The animals seem to be dreadfully afraid of me," the old man said as he entered, "and I am so fond of them." Again his teeth looked sharp and pointed, and his eyes were longer and greener than ever.

But Rosita's mother didn't seem to notice. She had never

turned anyone away from her door, and she was pleased to offer the old man food and shelter for the night.

Rosita cooked the supper and placed it on the table while the old man and her mother talked together like old friends. Among the dishes was a small plate of stewed lamb which Rosita had purchased as a special treat for her mother. To her amazement, their guest suddenly snatched it from her mother's hand and ate the whole plateful.

"I am afraid of him," said Rosita's mother, after she had shown the stranger to his room.

"Why, I thought you liked him when he first came," Rosita answered.

"I did," said her mother, "but now I believe he is dangerous, and it is too late to turn him out. You must keep watch with those," and she pointed to some firearms that hung over the fireplace in the kitchen.

Rosita's peace of mind was broken for the night, and she was determined to stay up. If nothing happened, so much the better. But if anything did occur, she would be ready.

It was a terrible night outside. The wind blew in great gusts, and the snow fell thick and fast, covering the ground for miles around with a heavy white blanket. In spite of the weather, however, Rosita went to the kennel and brought Moro into the house. The dog was only too glad to get into a snug warm place, and he lay down quietly before the fire in the kitchen. Then Rosita hunted up the little kitten who came from under the bed most willingly. Moro and the kitten ate their supper near the fire, and she shut up the house for the night.

After some time, Rosita closed the kitchen door because it was cold, and took down her father's old-fashioned blunderbuss and loaded it. The kitten lay on her lap while Moro rested at her feet, and soon Rosita fell sound asleep.

Suddenly Moro woke her with a terrible howl. The kitten was spitting and crying on her knee, and she saw by the light of the small oil lamp that the kitchen door was wide open. A huge wolf was standing in the doorway, his green, narrow eyes glaring, his teeth pointed, all ready for a spring. In a moment Rosita fired the gun, and the wolf fell to the floor.

But as she drew near, she was startled to see the old man—not the wolf—who lay mortally wounded. His green eyes were half closed, and his sharp teeth were barely visible as he moved his lips in an effort to speak. Looking up into her face he gasped, "You have done me a real kindness in ridding me of this dreadful life, and I thank you."

Early the next morning a farmer knocked at Rosita's door. "I have come to warn you about a gigantic wolf," said he.

"The wolf!" exclaimed Rosita.

"Yes," said the man, "the most vicious beast I've ever seen—with green eyes and sharp pointed teeth. It has killed many of my flocks and those of my neighbors as well. I know your father is away, so you must take great care."

"It was kind of you to travel so many miles to warn me," Rosita answered, "but I believe the wolf has met his fate at last."

And so he had. The werewolf was gone forever.

RICHMUTH
OF
COLOGNE

Barbara Leonie Picard

I n Cologne, in the middle ages, there lived a rich burgo-master whose much-loved wife was named Richmuth. One sad day Richmuth was seized by a sudden sick-ness, so that she fell to the ground and lay still and cold as though she were dead. The burgomaster sent for the best doctors in the city, but all to no avail, for none of them could help her, and each one shook his head and said, "There is nothing I can do. Your wife is dead."

Richmuth was laid in her coffin; and as her heartbroken husband took his last farewell of her, he put on her cold finger a favorite ring of hers which had been his gift to her and which she had often worn. When the members of his household sought to prevent him, saying that the ring should surely be kept, along with her other jewelry, for her children, he answered, "It was her favorite jewel. I did not lend it to her to wear for a few years. I gave it to her forever. Let her take it with her." And he would not listen to their protests.

The coffin was carried to the church and Richmuth was buried, and sadly the burgomaster returned home alone. But before the lid of the coffin had been closed, the sexton had noticed the ring on Richmuth's finger and he had thought to himself, "It is a shame that such a costly ring should be left hidden below the earth. It would fetch a good price, were it sold." His regrets quickly turned to longing, and his longing to a determination to possess the ring. All day he thought of nothing else, and at midnight he stole silently from his house, went to the church, opened the grave and pried off the lid of the coffin.

There, on Richmuth's finger, was the ring, glinting in the light of the lantern he had brought with him. Covetously he stretched out his hand to take it. But even as he did so, he saw her hand move and grope and take hold of the side of the coffin, as though the dead woman would raise herself up. Terrified, the sexton dropped his lantern, so that it went out, and fled.

Now, Richmuth had not really been dead, but only in a deep trance, and at the moment when the sexton had opened the coffin, she had come to herself again. She sat up in the darkness, wondering where she was and what had befallen her. When she felt the winding sheet about her and saw the tall shape of the church towering above her, she guessed what had happened. Quickly she unwound the grave clothes and stood up. "My poor husband," she thought, "how unhappy he will be, believing me dead. And my children will be needing me."

Stumbling, for she was very weak from her illness, she made her way to the street, her one thought to reach her home as quickly as she might. The streets were dark and deserted, and there was no one about who might have helped her. Shivering with the cold, she hurried past the sleeping houses, and at last, after what seemed to her a lifetime's journey, exhausted and well nigh as cold as though she had really been a corpse, she reached her home, and found the big house door barred against her.

She beat on the door with her fists and called till she was hoarse; and at last, by luck, one of the servingmen heard her, came to the door, opened it an inch or two and looked out. "Who are you, disturbing a house of mourning with such unseemly noise, and at this hour of the night?" he asked.

"It is I, Johannes, your mistress. For the love of God, let me in."

He held up the lantern he had lighted and peered at her. Her face was white and her hair disheveled, but it was his mistress all right. And, what is more, she was alive and no ghost. Yet, he thought, how could she be alive, for had he not seen her buried that morning, and wept for her, too?

"I can see it is you, mistress," he said. "Yet how can it be you? For you were buried this morning."

"It is I, it is I, Johannes. Let me in," she pleaded.

But he was far from being the most quick-witted of the burgomaster's servants, and he just stood there, holding the door open barely a crack, wrinkling his brows and trying to puzzle it out. And it was more than his wits could manage to decide what he should do. "I shall go and ask the master," he said to himself. "He will know what I ought to do." So he pushed the door to and hurried off up the stairs to the burgomaster's bedchamber.

Poor Richmuth, whose only comfort all through the dark, cold and endless-seeming walk through the city, had been the thought of the welcome she would receive when she reached home, and the great happiness of her husband and her children and all the household, could bear no more. She could not even make the effort to push open the door and walk in. She sank to the ground beside the doorpost, covered her face with her hands and wept.

In his bedchamber the burgomaster lay unsleeping, too sunk in grief to have heard the knocking on the door. "What do you want, Johannes?" he asked, when the servant came in.

"Are you awake, master?"

"What do you want?"

"The mistress is at the door, master. She is asking to come in. What am I to do?"

The burgomaster sat up in bed. "You are dreaming, man. Or else you have gone out of your mind."

"I am wide awake, master; the mistress woke me with her knocking. And I am in my right mind, but very puzzled as to what I should do. Am I to let her in?"

The burgomaster was too unhappy even to be angry. "If this is some cruel jest," he said, "then may God forgive those who are playing it on me."

"It is no jest, master. The mistress is standing outside the door. Am I to let her in?"

The burgomaster lay back upon the pillows. "I would as soon believe that my horses would come out of the stable and into the house through the door, and walk up the stairs to this room, as that my Richmuth were standing outside." He turned his head away and wept.

The servant stood in the middle of the room, holding

his lantern and scratching his head and wondering. The master had failed him. He had not told him what to do. And if the master had not told him, who was there left to ask?

Then suddenly he heard the clattering of hoofs from the hall below and then a trampling on the stairway, and he ran from the room with his lantern to see. There, coming up the stairs side by side, were his master's two white horses.

He ran back to the bedchamber, barely able to speak for excitement. "Master, master, the horses are coming up the stairs!"

The burgomaster raised his head. "You are mad," he said. But then he could hear it, too, hoofs clattering on the wooden stairway and then a loud triumphant neighing as they reached the top. He sprang out of bed, never stopped to pull on his boots or to put on a bedgown, but snatched the lantern from the servant and ran out of the room, giving no more than a glance at the horses outside his door, and was away down the stairs and across the hall.

The house door stood wide open where the horses had passed through, and at first it seemed as though there were no one outside. And then he saw her, huddled on the ground beside the doorpost, weeping. "Richmuth," he said, "Richmuth." And a moment later she was safe in his arms.

They lived together in joy and happiness for many years more; and, in memory of that night, the burgomaster had two carved horses' heads set upon his house wall.

THE
GOLDEN
COCKEREL

Ida Zeitlin

L ong ago, before the days of thy great-grandsire or of his grandsire, the illustrious Tsar Dadón ruled his tsardom and guarded it against invasion. And if his enemies dared oppose him, he girt his shining sword about him and went forth into battle. Then he fell upon them with so great a slaughter that none remained alive save only one, whom the Tsar spared that he might return to his country and bear with him the tale of the prowess of Dadón. All the neighboring rulers trembled at his name, and all the princes acclaimed him and bowed down before him. Whatever affront Dadón chose to put upon them, they had to suffer it in silence.

But the years came and withered his arm and dulled his eye. His head grew heavy with the weight of his power

and his shoulders drooped under their burden. Fain was
he to abandon the rigors of warfare for ease and soft living,
but his vigilant foes, biding their hour in the day of his
strength, saw now that the day of his weakness was upon
him. Straightway they assembled their armies and harried
him upon all his borders, laying waste his lands and plun-
dering his people and spreading desolation in their wake.
Dadón scourged his weary limbs to the attack. He multi-
plied his legions until their number was so great that none
remained to till the soil or keep the vineyards, and a famine
was over all the land.

And still he knew not how he should prevail over his
adversary. For though his soldiers fought bravely and
bravely perished, Dadón was confounded by the hordes of
his enemy as a weary steed by the blows of a savage rider.
Did he ride southward, swift couriers hastened to him
with tidings that an armed force approached from the
west. Did he turn westward, a flourish of trumpets
sounded the alarm in the east. And Dadón knew neither
joy in the morning nor peace at night.

Wherefore he sent his criers throughout the country to
proclaim that whosoever should find a way to destroy the
enemy, upon him would Dadón heap honors and a mountain of golden rubles.

A day and a night passed, and a second day and a night,
and on the evening of the third day an ancient sorcerer
passed through the city and came before the throne of the
Tsar. Black was his raiment, and white his beard as the
breast of a swan. His face was withered as a dry leaf,
and his eyes burned like coals in the gray ashes of a fire.
In his right hand he bore a bag from the depths of which
he drew forth a golden cockerel and offered it to Dadón.

"Majesty," said he, "thy word hath traveled even to that dusty corner of the earth wherein thy servant plies his humble arts. Behold this golden cockerel that I have fashioned for thy need. Faithful is he and vigilant and bold. Let him be set upon a pinnacle atop the loftiest dome of thy golden palace, and thou shalt need no other sentinel. For while thy foes lie harmless within their strongholds, he will rest motionless upon his height. But let the wind bear to him over the mountains the lightest breath of their approach—be it from the deserts of the west or from the southern seas or from the perfumed bazaars of the Orient —and my golden bird will ruffle his plumage, raise his crest and, turning in the direction whence danger threatens, cry, 'Kiri-ku-ku,' in tones so sweet and shrill that they must reach thine ears, O Majesty, though thou wert buried beneath the snows of fifty winters."

Dadón took the golden bird in his hand and laughed with pleasure, saying, "O sage and saviour of my tsardom, thou who hast served a prince shalt have a prince's reward. A mountain of gold shall be thine and a river of silver. And whatsoever thy desire may be, either now or in the fullness of time, it shall be as my own desire and naught shall stay its fulfillment. This pledge do I pledge thee."

"As for gold and silver, Sire, what need have I of these, who am content with black bread for my hunger and clear water for my thirst? And as for my desires, they are not as the desires of other men. Yet who can say what lies hidden in the stars? It may be that one day I shall return to redeem thy pledge." So saying, the sorcerer bowed his head thrice to the ground, turned and left the palace and was seen no more.

At once the Tsar ordered that the golden cockerel be set upon a pinnacle atop the loftiest dome of his palace. And while his enemies lay harmless within their strongholds, the little bird slumbered upon his height. But with the first stir of strife, however distant and however secret, he awoke, ruffled his golden plumage, raised his golden crest and, turning in the direction whence danger threatened, cried, "Kiri-ku-ku! Kiri-ku-ku! Kiri-ku-koooo!" So sweet and shrill were his tones that whether Dadón walked in the garden or galloped afar in the chase, he heard the golden bird and led his legions against the enemy. He mowed them down and scattered them to the four winds, so that his glory was proclaimed anew and none dared cross swords with him.

Thus did the golden bird keep watch over the tsardom, and Dadón arose in the morning with a quiet heart and with an untroubled spirit laid him down at nightfall. And peace dwelt upon his borders.

Three joyful years passed, and as the fourth year dawned, Dadón lay one night in tranquil slumber. Yet it seemed to him that a faint far cry disturbed his rest, but so sweetly did he slumber that he gave it no heed, and did but sigh and draw the purple coverlet closer about his head. And a sudden tumult arose in the city streets and drew nigh the palace walls and grew in volume and in fury. And the Tsar awoke and cried, "Who dares to disturb the slumber of Dadón the Tsar!"

The voice of the commander of his army called to him, "Thou, O Tsar, father and defender of thy people, awake! Disaster is upon us. Awake, O Tsar, and look to thy tsardom!"

"Get ye back to your beds, ye foolish ones," cried

Dadón, "and be at peace! Know ye not that the golden cockerel sleeps and no harm can come nigh ye?"

"The golden cockerel wakes, Sire, and cries to the west, and thy people clamor to thee for protection."

Dadón looked from the window to where the golden cockerel kept watch on his lofty pinnacle. And he saw that the bird beat his wings in frenzy and turned ever toward the west. And even as he gazed, the cockerel raised his golden crest and cried, "Kiri-ku-ku! Kiri-ku-ku! Kiri-ku-koooo!"

Thereupon the Tsar donned his royal crown and took his royal scepter and went forth from the palace. He commanded that an army be assembled, at whose head he placed his elder son, known through the length and breadth of the land as Igor the Valiant. Him he kissed upon either cheek and bade godspeed, saying, "For the head of mine enemy half my kingdom."

And Igor the Valiant answered, "Thine enemy is mine, O Sire and Tsar," and mounted his steel-gray steed and rode away to the west. And his troops rode behind him. The golden cockerel grew silent upon his pinnacle, and the Tsar's people returned to their homes. Dadón lay down upon his royal couch and fell into tranquil slumber.

Thus passed eight days, and Dadón awaited tidings of the battle and of his son Igor. But though he gazed from his window until his eyes grew dim, no heralds approached from the west nor could he learn aught of what had befallen.

Suddenly the golden cockerel on his pinnacle awoke, ruffled his plumage, turned toward the west and cried, "Kiri-ku-ku! Kiri-ku-ku! Kiri-ku-koooo!"

And again a murmur arose among the dwellers in the

city and the murmur grew to a roar, and again they surrounded the palace of Dadón and prayed to him for protection.

Thereupon the Tsar commanded that a second army be assembled, outnumbering the army of Igor the Valiant by a thousand legions, and at its head he placed his younger son, known far and wide as Oleg the Magnificent. Him he kissed upon either cheek and bade godspeed, saying, "For the head of mine enemy half my kingdom."

And Oleg the Magnificent answered, "Thine enemy is mine, O Sire and Tsar," and mounted his milk-white steed and rode away to the west. And his troops rode behind him. The golden cockerel grew silent upon his pinnacle and the people returned to their homes, and Dadón slept.

Thus passed eight days, and Dadón watched the western sky for the first sight of the couriers of his son Oleg. But though he watched till his lids grew weary, there came neither courier nor any word from those who had gone forth to do battle with the Tsar's enemies.

The heart of Dadón grew heavy with dread, and the people crept away into hidden places, and when they went forth, they went in terror. And suddenly the golden cockerel on his pinnacle awoke. He ruffled his plumage, turned toward the west, raised his crest and cried, "Kiri-ku-ku! Kiri-ku-ku! Kiri-ku-koooo!"

Now the Tsar commanded a third army to be assembled, outnumbering the armies of Igor the Valiant and Oleg the Magnificent by countless legions. He girt his shining sword about him, mounted his night-black steed, and rode away to the west. His troops rode behind him, and gray care rode by his side.

Onward they journeyed toward the setting sun, and

the night fell and the dawn broke, and a second night and a second dawn, and still they rode without pause. And though they scanned earth and sky to north and south, they saw neither the pitched tents of their friends nor the burial mounds of their enemies nor any blood-scarred battlefields.

"Surely this is an omen," thought Dadón, "but whether of good or evil who can tell me?"

Onward they journeyed through the dawn and the noon and the night. The soldiers slept in their saddles and their horses stumbled for weariness. Seven days they journeyed and seven nights, and on the evening of the eighth day they came within sight of the purple hills and through a cleft in the hills they beheld a silken tent.

"It is the tent of mine enemy," said Dadón. And over hills and valleys a deep silence lay.

And so they approached the cleft. Before it lay the body of one who had ridden with Igor the Valiant, and a great wound gaped in his side. Close by lay the body of one who had followed Oleg the Magnificent, and his head was struck from his shoulders. Dadón looked about him and saw naught but the lifeless bodies of his soldiers . . . but his sons he saw not.

Then he drew his sword from its sheath and rode toward the silken tent of his enemy. But his steed trembled and would bear him no farther. In the distance he beheld the steeds of his two sons and they galloped to and fro in their madness. But his sons he saw not.

Then he alighted and went on foot toward the silken tent and before its portal he paused. For there he saw his sons, their shields cast from them, and the naked blade of each was lodged in the heart of his brother.

The Tsar flung himself upon the earth and rent his garments and lifted his voice in a loud lament. "Woe, woe is me!" he cried. "Both my bright falcons snared in an evil net! Your death is mine, my sons, that should have lived to mourn for me!"

And all the hosts of his army wept with him, so that the very depths of the valleys trembled and the heart of the mountains was shaken with their cries.

Suddenly the portal of the tent was raised, and a maiden stepped forth whose beauty was as the beauty of the young dawn and of the radiant sun and of the shining stars. And when the Tsar beheld her, he was as one bereft of the power of movement, and his heart grew quiet as a night bird at the break of day. And she smiled upon him, and straightway he forgot whence he had come or wherefore; the memory of his two sons was strange to him. For her beauty blinded the sight of men and ravished their hearts, so that all dear and familiar things grew alien. None could withstand the potency of her spell.

She bowed her head before him and took his hand. And she led him into her tent and placed before him a table laden with rare foods and crimson wines. And he looked into her eyes and said, "The tent of mine enemy have I sought, and found the tent of my beloved."

She smiled but spake no word, and anointed his limbs with fragrant oils and laid him to rest upon a couch of swansdown and covered him with a cloth of gold. And she sat beside him and played sweet music on a golden lute, and Dadón slumbered.

For eight days he dwelt with her in her tent, and ate and drank plentifully and slept softly, and knew not weariness nor regret. But on the evening of the eighth day he commanded that a chariot be brought, drawn by four stallions, and he said to the maiden, "Now shalt thou come with me to my golden palace which is eight days' journey from this place, and dwell with me there in love and joy as I have dwelt with thee in thy silken tent." And she stepped into the chariot and Dadón sat beside her, and her hand lay in his as a bird in its nest.

At length they came within sight of the city gates, and the people of Dadón came forth to meet them with shouting and revelry. For the tidings of what had befallen had gone before them, and the people rejoiced that the golden cockerel slept on his pinnacle. Their Tsar who had ridden forth in peril had returned in safety, and with him was a Tsarevna who was the most beautiful in all the tsardoms of the earth.

The heart of Dadón grew big with pride, and he bowed to this side and to that and doffed his plumed hat, returning the greetings of his people. And the maiden smiled upon them.

But suddenly the throng parted, and the ancient sorcerer appeared before the chariot of the Tsar. Black was his raiment and white his beard as the breast of a swan. His face was withered as a dry leaf and his eyes burned like coals in the gray ashes of a fire.

And the Tsar greeted him, crying, "Health to thee, venerable father! And to the golden cockerel life without end! Peace hath he brought to my kingdom, and to mine arms my beloved."

The sorcerer bowed his head three times to the ground and answered, "Well for me, Majesty, that he hath found favor in thy sight. For I am come to redeem thy pledge. For the service of the golden cockerel thou didst swear that my desire should be as thy desire and naught should stay its fulfillment."

"It is the word of the Tsar."

"Give me then the maiden for my bride."

Then Dadón arose from his place, and his eyes flashed flame and his voice rolled like thunder behind the hills. And upon all the shouting multitude a deep silence fell.

"Thou fool and knave! What madness is this? What fiend of darkness hath seized thee to turn thy wisdom to folly and thine honor to shame?"

"It is thy word, Sire."

"Yet have all things their measure, and the maid is not for thee."

"So is the Tsar forsworn."

"And were he twenty times forsworn, thou shouldst not have her. Gold is thine for the asking, more than ten men can carry—the rarest of wines from the royal store—the swiftest stallion from the stables of the Tsar—rank and honor and broad lands will I give thee even unto the half of my tsardom. Thou shalt be second to none save the Tsar alone."

"My desire is for neither land nor riches, nor for honors nor swift steeds nor rare wines. My desire is for the maid. Do thou according to thy word and yield her up to me."

Then did the Tsar's wrath wax exceeding great, and he spat upon the garment of the ancient man and cried, "Begone from my sight lest harm befall thee!"

But the sorcerer would not move, and Dadón cried, "Let him be taken away!"

And two soldiers stepped forward, but when they tried to seize the sorcerer, their arms fell powerless to their sides.

Once again the sorcerer cried, "It is thy word, Sire . . ." But Dadón raised aloft his golden scepter and smote the ancient man upon the brow, and he fell upon the ground. His black garments covered him and his spirit left his body.

Then did the Tsar's people avert their eyes one from the other, for they were troubled by a foreboding of evil. And the heart of Dadón was heavy with the weight of his sin. But the maiden, who knew not good nor evil, parted her red lips and laughed long and merrily, and Dadón, listening, was comforted. So they journeyed into the city and the body of the ancient sorcerer lay by the wayside.

As they neared the palace gates, there sounded a sudden whirring as of the beat of wings, and in sight of all the multitude the golden cockerel flew from his pinnacle and lit upon the head of Tsar Dadón. Every eye was fixed on him but no hand was raised to succor him, for all were bound as by the power of some strange enchantment.

And the golden cockerel drove his beak once through the head of Dadón and cried, "Kiri-ku-ku! Kiri-ku-ku! Kiri-ku-kooo!" and spread his golden wings and flew away beyond the knowledge and the sight of men.

But Dadón fell to the ground, groaned once and died.

As for the maiden, she vanished like a dream that is done.

THE
SEAL CATCHER
AND
THE MERMAN

Elizabeth W. Grierson

ONCE there was a man who lived not very far from John o' Groat's house which, as everyone knows, is in the very north of Scotland. He lived in a little cottage by the seashore and made his living by catching seals and selling their fur.

He earned a good deal of money in this way, for these creatures used to come out of the sea in large numbers. They lay on the rocks near his house basking in the sunshine, so it was not difficult to creep up from behind and kill them.

Some of the seals were larger than others, and the country people used to call them "Roane," and whisper that they were not seals at all but mermen and merwomen who came from a country of their own far down under the ocean. They assumed this strange disguise in order to pass through the water and come up to breathe the air of the earth.

But the seal catcher only laughed at such ideas. He said that those seals were most worth killing, for their skins were so big he got an extra price for them.

Now it chanced one day, when he was pursuing his calling that he stabbed a seal with his hunting knife. Perhaps his stroke had not been sure enough, but with a loud cry of pain the creature slipped off the rock and disappeared under the water carrying the knife along with it.

The seal catcher, much annoyed at his clumsiness, and also at the loss of his knife, started home in a very downcast frame of mind. On his way he met a horesman who was so tall and so strange looking and who rode on such a gigantic horse that he stopped and looked at him in astonishment, wondering who he was and from what country he came.

The stranger stopped also and asked him his trade. On hearing that he was a seal catcher, he immediately ordered a great number of seal skins. The seal catcher was delighted, for such an order meant a large sum of money. But his face fell when the horseman added that it was absolutely necessary that the skins be delivered that evening.

"I cannot do it," he said in a disappointed voice, "for the seals will not come back to the rocks again until morning."

"I can take you to a place where there are any number of seals," answered the stranger, "if you will mount behind me on my horse and come with me."

The seal catcher agreed to this. He climbed up behind the rider who shook his bridle rein, and off the great horse galloped at such a pace that he had much ado to keep his seat.

On and on they went, flying like the wind, until at last they came to the edge of a huge precipice, the face of which went sheer down to the sea. Here the mysterious horseman pulled up his steed with a jerk.

"Get off now," he said shortly.

The seal catcher did as he was bid, and when he found himself safe on the ground, he peeped cautiously over the edge of the cliff to see if there were any seals lying on the rocks below.

To his astonishment he saw no rocks, only the blue sea which came right up to the foot of the cliff.

"Where are the seals that you spoke of?" he asked anxiously, wishing that he had never set out on such a rash adventure.

"You will see presently," answered the stranger, who was attending to his horse's bridle.

The seal catcher was now thoroughly frightened, for he felt sure that some evil was about to befall him. In such a lonely place he knew that it would be useless to cry out for help.

And it seemed as if his fears would prove only too true. The next moment the stranger's hand was laid upon his shoulder, and the seal catcher felt himself being hurled over the cliff, and then he fell with a splash into the sea.

He thought that his last hour had come, and he wondered how anyone could work such a deed of wrong upon an innocent man.

But to his amazement, he found that some change must have passed over him for instead of being choked by the water, he could breathe quite easily. And he and his companion, who was still close at his side, seemed to be sinking as quickly down through the sea as they had flown through the air.

Down and down they went, nobody knows how far, till at last they came to an arched door made of pink coral, studded over with cockleshells. It opened of its own accord, and when they entered they found themselves in a huge hall. The walls were formed of mother-of-pearl, and the floor was of sea sand, smooth, and firm, and yellow.

The hall was crowded with occupants, but they were seals, not men. And when the seal catcher turned to his companion to ask what it all meant, he was aghast to find that he, too, had assumed the form of a seal. But he was most horrified when he caught sight of himself in a large mirror that hung on the wall. No longer did he bear the likeness of a man. He had been transformed into a furry, brown seal!

"Ah, woe is me," he said to himself, "for no fault of my own this stranger has laid some baneful charm upon me, and in this awful guise will I remain for the rest of my natural life."

At first none of the huge creatures spoke to him. For some reason or other they seemed to be very sad, and moved gently about the hall talking quietly and mournfully to one another, or lay upon the sandy floor wiping big tears from their eyes.

But presently they began to notice him, and to whisper to one another, and soon his guide moved away from him. He disappeared through a door at the end of the hall, and when he returned he held a huge knife in his hand.

"Did you ever see this before?" he asked the unfortunate seal catcher who, to his horror, recognized his own hunting knife with which he had struck the seal in the morning, and which had been carried off by the wounded animal.

At the sight of it he fell upon his face and begged for mercy, for he at once concluded that the inhabitants of the cavern, enraged at the harm which had been wrought upon their comrade, had, in some magic way, contrived to capture him and wreak their vengeance by killing him.

But instead of doing so, they crowded round him, rubbing their noses against his fur to show their sympathy. They assured him that no harm would befall him; they would be grateful all their lives if he would only do what they asked.

"Tell me what it is," said the seal catcher, "and I will do it if it lies within my power."

"Follow me," answered his guide, and he led the way to the door through which he had disappeared when he went to seek the knife.

The seal catcher followed him. And there, in a smaller room, he found a great brown seal lying on a bed of pale green seaweed, with a gaping wound in his side.

"That is my father," said his guide, "whom you wounded this morning. You thought he was one of the common seals who live in the sea, instead of a merman who has speech and understanding as you mortals have. I brought you here to bind up his wounds, for no other hand than yours can heal him."

"I have no skill in the art of healing," said the seal catcher, astonished at the forbearance of these strange creatures whom he had so unwittingly wronged. "But I will bind up the wound to the best of my power, and I am only sorry that it was my hands that caused it."

He went over to the bed and, stooping over the injured merman, washed and dressed the wound as well as he could. His touch appeared to work like magic, for no sooner had he finished than the wound seemed to heal, leaving only a scar. The old seal sprang up as well as ever.

Then there was great rejoicing throughout the whole Palace of the Seals. They laughed, and they talked, and they embraced each other in their own strange way. They crowded round their comrade, rubbing their noses against his as if to show how delighted they were at his recovery.

But the seal catcher stood alone in a corner with his mind filled with dark thoughts. Although he saw now that they had no intention of killing him, he did not relish the prospect of spending the rest of his life in the guise of a seal, fathoms deep under the ocean.

But presently his guide approached him and said, "Now you are at liberty to return home to your wife and children. I will take you to them, but only on one condition."

"And what is that?" asked the seal catcher, overjoyed at the prospect of being restored safely to the upper world, and to his family.

"That you will take a solemn oath never to wound a seal again."

"That will I do right gladly," he replied, for although the promise meant giving up his means of livelihood, he felt that if only he regained his proper shape, he could always turn his hand to something else.

So he took the required oath with all due solemnity, holding up his flipper as he swore, and all the others seals crowded round him as witnesses. And a sigh of relief went through the halls when the words were spoken, for he was the most noted seal catcher in the North.

Then he bade the strange company farewell and, accompanied by his guide, passed once more through the outer doors of coral, and up and up and up through the shadowy green water until it began to grow lighter and lighter, and they finally emerged into the sunshine of the earth.

Then, with one spring, they reached the top of the cliff, where the great black horse was waiting for them, quietly nibbling the green turf.

When they left the water, their strange disguise dropped from them. They were now as they had been before—a plain seal catcher and a tall, well-dressed gentleman in riding clothes.

"Get up behind me," said the latter as he swung himself into his saddle. The seal catcher did as he was bid, taking tight hold of his companion's coat, for he remembered how he had nearly fallen off on his previous journey.

Then it all happened as it happened before. The bridle was shaken and the horse galloped off, and it was not long before the seal catcher found himself standing in safety before his own garden gate.

He held out his hand to say "good-by," but as he did so, the stranger pulled out a huge bag of gold and placed it in his palms.

"You have done your part; we must do ours," he said. "No one shall ever say that we took away an honest man's work without making reparation for it. Here is what will keep you in comfort to your life's end."

Then he vanished, and the astonished seal catcher carried the bag into his cottage. When he turned the gold out on the table, he found that what the stranger had said was true. He would be a rich man for the remainder of his days.

THE BIRD
THAT WOULD NOT
STAY DEAD

Frances Carpenter

S TRANGE things happened in ancient times. Or so it would seem from stories out of the past in Africa. And nothing, you must admit, could be more strange than a bird that sang with man's words and would not stay dead.

This story comes from the part of South Africa where most of the people belong to a Kaffir tribe. Round Kaffir huts, with their roofs of dried grass, have the shape of upside-down bowls. Together, a group of these bowl-shaped huts forms a village known as a kraal.

In one Kaffir kraal, long, long ago, there lived a certain man whose name we may call Bunu. Two huts he had, one for each of his wives. His Great Wife, of course, was the one he had married first. She should have been happy.

She had two fine sons, and that gave her much honor in her husband's mind.

But his Great Wife was jealous of Bunu's Small Wife. Why should she have been jealous? It was the custom for important men of that kraal to have two wives, or even more. The second, or Small Wife, did not share the Great Wife's hut. She had a hut of her own.

Bunu's Small Wife was young. She was prettier, too. The Small Wife was stronger. She could grind the corn faster. She could bring in upon her head more wood from the forest. And she was quicker to gather it. Her husband praised her often. It was clear he loved her well.

One day the two women were out in the forest gathering firewood for Bunu's cooking fires. They worked all the morning. But when afternoon came, they decided to rest a while.

It was then that the honey guide came to the Small Wife. The small gray-brown bird chattered as it flew about the girl's head. Then it darted a little way off into the forest.

"It's a honey guide, Sister," the Small Wife called out in delight to the Great Wife. "It will show me the way to a honey bee tree."

She ran after the bird. And, as she had said, it led her straight to a tree where a swarm of bees had their nest. This African bird is well known for its own love of honey. Some say when it chatters, it is asking for help in getting the comb out of the tree.

The Small Wife was sure that the bird came to find her because of a bird-feather charm which she always wore. It had been made for her out of the feathers of a honey guide, by the witch doctor of her own kraal. She was sure its magic was strong. She kept it always, tied into one of her necklaces of beads.

So swiftly did the Small Wife run after the honey guide that she had already taken the comb out of the tree when the Great Wife came to her. The younger wife was a kind person. She was glad to share her find with the other.

"Here is some honey for you, Sister," the Small Wife said. "I must give some to the little bird that showed me this nest. Then, from my own part, I must save some to take home to our husband."

These words did not please the Great Wife at all. Her husband loved honey. He would praise the Small Wife because she had found the bee tree and brought its honey home to him.

When the Small Wife was not looking, the wicked woman stole the honey which the girl had wrapped up in a fresh green leaf for Bunu. That's how it happened that, when they were ready to go home, the Small Wife could not find any honey at all.

"Perhaps a jackal stole it," the Great Wife nodded her head.

"Perhaps!" the Small Wife answered. She had no thought that the older woman would play such a mean trick.

At home, that evening, Bunu came first to the hut of his Great Wife. He was pleased with her present of the honeycomb. And he praised her for finding the honey bee tree.

The jealous woman did not tell him the true story. She did not say that it was the Small Wife who had gathered the sweet comb.

Bunu hurried off then to the hut of his other wife. No

doubt, he thought, she, being younger, would have brought him even more honey. But she only showed him the huge pile of firewood she had carried home on her head.

"Have you no honey for me, Wife?" Bunu asked her. "Or did you eat it all up yourself?" This was not kind, and the Small Wife hung her head.

"I found the bee tree, my husband. And I wrapped all my comb in a green leaf to bring home to you. I gave your Great Wife a tiny bit to eat herself, and I left a taste for the honey guide who showed me the way to the tree. All the rest I had saved for you. But some animal stole it."

"Your mouth is big. You boast of things you did not do." Her husband spoke too quickly. He should have re-membered that the Great Wife had honey tied up in a green leaf.

"My Great Wife says that it was she who found the bee's nest. If it was you, as you say, you would surely have brought some honey away with you." Oh, that man was not kind.

Bunu seized the poor girl by the neck. Her strings of beads broke. All of her lucky charms fell to the ground, including the one made of honey-guide feathers. She had no magic now to protect her.

Oh, Bunu was a cruel man. His anger was fierce. And that was no doubt because, when he was a boy, his father had fed him upon the heart of a lion.

In his awful rage, and with no magic to stop him, he killed his Small Wife. It was in the dark of the night. No one at all saw him when he buried her in the ground under her hut.

So dark it was in the hut that Bunu himself did not see what took place then on the earth floor of the hut. The

Small Wife's feather charm began to move about on the ground. How could her husband guess that his young wife's own spirit had gone into the charm? Even when the charm turned into a bird and flew out the door, the man thought it was a wind which had blown the feathers away.

With his wife gone, wicked Bunu thought of the oxen he had paid as her bride price.

"I will go to her father. I will tell him his daughter is no longer my wife. I will ask for my oxen. And he will have to give them back to me when he sees she is not in my hut."

Bunu was on the road to the kraal of his Small Wife's family. And suddenly a little gray-brown bird began to fly around and around his head. He heard wailing music, but he thought it was only the sound of wind blowing through the bird's lyre-shaped tail. The stiff tail feathers of the honey guide were shaped like an ancient harp. Music often came from them when the bird flew fast through the air.

But now there were words along with the wailing music. Clear and loud the man heard them. And he could scarcely believe his ears.

> *"I am the Spirit*
> *Of Bunu's Small Wife.*
>
> *"Just for some honey,*
> *He took my life."*

Bunu was frightened. It would never do to let this bird sing that song where anyone else might hear. He took out his throwing stick. And he knocked the small gray-brown bird down on the ground. In a hole in the earth he buried the dead bird. Then, feeling safer, he went on his way.

He had not gone far, however, when the honey guide was back again. Flying around and around his head! Keeping out of his reach! And singing as before!

> *"I am the Spirit*
> *Of Bunu's Small Wife.*
>
> *"Just for some honey,*
> *He took my life."*

"This time I will make sure that the cursed bird will stay dead," the frightened man then said to himself. "No one else must hear this tattletale bird sing this song." And when his throwing stick had knocked it down again, he put the dead bird inside his tobacco pouch. He tied the bag tight. And he hung it from his own belt.

Bunu was not worried now. When he came to the kraal of the family of his Small Wife, a feast was going on. People were singing and dancing. Drums were beating. There was food and drink for all the guests.

"Come dance with us, Bunu," his Small Wife's father welcomed him. "How is our dear daughter? Why have you left her at home?"

"We will speak of her later," said Bunu, brushing the question aside. He loved singing and dancing. And he felt safe. The unfeeling man joined in the merriment. No one would have guessed from his actions that he had killed his Small Wife.

But at last, her father pulled Bunu out of the dance.

"We will talk now, Bunu. Tell me of my daughter. Why are you here without her?"

"Your daughter is gone from my hut. She is no longer my wife." Bunu tried to look unhappy. "I have come here for the oxen which I gave you as her bride price."

It was the custom in this Kaffir tribe. If a girl was no longer a wife to her husband, the price he had paid for her must be given back.

Of course, it was true that his Small Wife was no longer to be seen in his hut. But Bunu did not say how this happened to be so. He thought nobody would ever find out.

Bunu might well have been right. He might even have had his oxen back if his wife's father had not just then asked him for tobacco to smoke in his pipe.

Not thinking what he was doing, Bunu untied his tobacco bag. And before he could shut it again, the little gray-brown honey guide had darted out. No longer dead was this magic bird. It was flying and flying around the heads of the two men. And again it was singing its dreadful song.

> *"I am the Spirit*
> *Of Bunu's Small Wife.*
>
> *"Just for some honey,*
> *He took my life."*

Many heard the words. The little bird sang them loud and clear. Again and again, it added, "Yes, he took your daughter's life." And the Small Wife's father knew what it meant. Yet he gave the cruel man a chance to explain.

"I do not know what the bird means," Bunu shouted. "This bird cannot know. It was dark when I buried my Small Wife in the ground under her hut."

Well, you can guess what happened then. It is too awful to tell about. But no one in that Kaffir kraal, or in any other, ever saw Bunu again.

89

THE
KITCHEN POOKA

Patrick Kennedy

WHEN Mr. Corcoran was away in Dublin, the servants took care of his big house in the country all the same as if he was home. Well, they used to be frightened out of their lives, after going to their beds at night, with the banging of the kitchen door and the clattering of the fire irons, and the pots, and pans, and dishes.

One evening they sat up ever so long keeping one another in heart with stories about ghosts and pookas and other spirits, while the little scullery boy crept close to the hearth. And when he got tired listening to the stories, he fell fast asleep.

Well and good, after the servants were all gone, and the

fire raked up, the lad woke to the noise of the kitchen door opening and a trampling on the floor. He opened his eyes, and what should he see but a big gray donkey—a pooka sure enough!

After a little, the pooka looked about him and began scratching his ears as if he was quite tired. "I may as well begin first as last," says he.

The poor boy's teeth began to chatter in his head, for says he, "Now he's going to eat me."

But the pooka with the long ears and tail on him had something else to do. He put his foot close to the hearth and pushed the little boy away. The boy yelled with fright, but the pooka only thrust out his lower lip to show how little he valued the lad and went on about his business.

Well then, the pooka stirred up a fire, and he brought in a pail of water from the pump and filled a big pot that he put on the fire. Then he lay down till he heard the water coming to a boil. And there wasn't a pot or a pan or a dish that he didn't put into the water and wash and dry as well as e'er a kitchen maid from there to Dublin town. He then put all of them up in their places on the shelves and gave a good sweeping to the kitchen floor.

Then he came and sat near the boy; he let down one of his ears, cocked up the other, and gave a grin. The poor lad strove to yell, but not a sound came out of his throat.

The last thing the pooka did was to rake up the fire and walk out. He gave such a slap o' the door that the boy thought the house couldn't help tumbling down.

Well, to be sure, if there wasn't a hullabulloo next morning when the poor fellow told his story! They could talk of nothing else the whole day. One said one thing, another said another. But they all agreed that a pooka doing household work was a most unheard of thing.

Still, a scullery girl named Kauth spoke the boldest words of all. "It may be unheard of," says she, "but that's no matter. If the pooka cleans up everything when we're asleep, why should we be slaving ourselves, doing his work!"

"Them's the wisest words you ever said, Kauth," says another, "and it's meself won't contradict you."

So said so done. Not a dish or a pot saw a drop of water that evening, and everyone went to bed soon after sundown. Next morning everything was as fine as fire in the kitchen, and the lord mayor could have eaten dinner off the floor. It was a great ease to the servants, you may be sure. And everything went well till bold Kauth said she would stay up one night and have a chat with the pooka.

She was a little daunted when the door was thrown open and the pooka marched up to the fire. Kauth didn't open her mouth till the pot was filled and the pooka lay snug by the fire.

"Ah then, sir," says she, at last picking up courage, "if it isn't taking a liberty, might I ask who you are, and why you are so kind as to do half of the day's work for us every night?"

"No liberty at all," says the pooka. "I'll tell you, and welcome. I was a servant here in the time of Squire Corcoran's father, and was the laziest rogue that ever was clothed and fed. When my time came for the other world, this is the punishment was laid on me—to come here and do labor every night, and then go out in the cold. It isn't so bad in the fine weather. But if you only knew what it is to stand with your head between your legs, facing a storm, from midnight to sunrise on a bleak winter night!"

"Could we do anything for your comfort, my poor fellow?" says Kauth.

"Musha, I don't know," says the pooka. "But I think a good quilted coat would help to keep the life in me through them long nights."

"Why then," says Kauth, "we'd be the most ungrateful people if we didn't feel for you."

To make a long story short, the next night Kauth was there again—and if she didn't delight the pooka with a fine warm coat! His legs got pushed into the four arms of it, and it was buttoned down his belly. The pooka was so pleased, he walked up to the glass to see how he looked.

"Well," says he, "it's a long lane that has no turning. I am much obliged to yourself and the others. You have made me happy at last. Good night to you."

So he was walking out, but Kauth cried, "Och! sure you're going too soon. What about the washing and sweeping?"

"Ah, you may tell the girls that they must now get their turn," says the pooka. "My punishment was to last till I was thought worthy of a reward for the way I did my duty. You'll see me no more."

And no more they did, and right sorry they were for being in such a hurry to reward the ungrateful pooka.

THE KNIGHT
WITH THE
STONE HEART

Roger Duvoisin

FROM his high castle on a wooded hill near Basle, the Knight of Waldenburg ruled over his soldiers, his peasants, and his servants. Whenever he rode over his lands everyone bowed with humility, but fear and hate were on every face, for the Lord of Waldenburg was a brutal and a cruel man. He was avaricious and made his peasants work beyond their strength. For pay he gave them scant food, and anyone so bold as to complain was flogged and thrown into the deep jails of Waldenburg castle.

Poor Hans, one of his peasants, daily grew more troubled at the bitterness of his lot. Finally he could bear no longer the unhappiness of coming home from a long day's work to find his hungry wife and children sitting around

97

a bare table, with only their meager ration of thin soup and coarse black bread before them.

"I am going to see our master," he told his wife. "I shall ask him for more food."

At that his wife began to wring her hands and cry. "Don't, Hans, don't. Remember what happened to our neighbor, Franz. He is now in the damp jail of Waldenburg. The same fate will be yours. Don't go, I implore you."

"I must," said poor Hans. "I can no longer bear to see our children starve." And with that he took one of the clay plates from the cupboard, and off he went to Waldenburg castle.

His heart beat fast as he passed the soldiers at the castle gate, standing sternly, armed with long spikes. His legs trembled a little as he was led into the dining room where the Knight of Waldenburg, in a thick scarlet coat, sat at dinner. He was devouring a leg of mutton. "What do you want, churl?" he growled, without looking up from his plate. "Speak out!"

"My wife and children starve," said Hans bravely. "I have come to demand food for them. I have always been a good laborer. I have done my share and more. But I cannot work any longer unless you fill this plate three times a day so that my family can eat." And he took the plate that he had been carrying, and held it out to the Knight of Waldenburg.

The Knight, in a fury, turned as red as his coat, and seizing the plate from Hans's hand, hurled it to the floor, where it broke into a thousand pieces.

"You don't want to work, you say?" he roared, striking the table with his fist. "Well, you won't have to. I'll put you in the place where you and your kind belong. Guards!

Take this man to the jail, where he can keep company with rats and spiders and his friend Franz."

In her wretched home, deep in the oak forest, Hans's wife waited the whole day for his return. From her small-paned window she watched the forest path that led to the castle, but except for a few red squirrels and a wild boar that crossed it rapidly, the path remained deserted.

Night fell.

Still Hans had not come.

Knowing her worst fears were realized, she spent the night in tears, trying to think of a way to save her husband.

In the morning they brought her the news that Hans had been put in jail. Drying her eyes, she stood up. "I shall go to see the Knight myself," she said. "He alone can release Hans and give food to my children."

Where the little forest path met the highway she came upon the fat Knight. Followed by a few servants he was taking his early morning walk, dressed in a heavy blue coat with sleeves as large as stove pipes, and on his head a small flat hat topped with a little feather, which made him look even fatter.

"My Lord," she said, kneeling down, "have pity on me and my poor Hans. The sight of his hungry children drove him to your castle to ask for food. Have pity. Release him. Give us the food we need."

For a while the Knight of Waldenburg stared at her silently. Then he picked up a stone from the side of the road, and offering it to her he said brutally, "Here is the bread you need. Go home, and when you have eaten, come back. I'll give you some more."

So angry that she was no longer afraid, Hans's wife rose to her feet. Taking the stone from the Knight's hand she brandished it in his face, and cried, "Your heart is like this stone. Oh, that it could turn your blood and body into a hard lifeless rock!"

Hardly had the words passed her lips when, to the astonishment of everyone present, a strange change came over the Knight. His face became pale and gray. His blue coat, his red hat and gold stockings seemed to lose their color. They became gray like his face. Stock-still he stood, with stony eyes staring fixedly ahead. He had indeed become a lifeless stone.

And there he remains to this day: a great rock by the wayside, reminding every passer-by of the fate of the cruel Knight of Waldenburg.

THE BOY IN THE SECRET VALLEY

Jón Arnason

IN a southern district of Iceland, there once lived a prosperous farmer and his wife who had only one son. He was a fine lad, dearly loved by his parents and, being their only child, he remained at home until he was sixteen.

One summer two neighboring farmers were going north to work as day laborers, and they asked the boy's parents if he could go with them. At first the farmer and his wife refused, but the boy was so eager to go that they finally gave their consent.

They provided their son with a good horse and a generous supply of food. Then the lad bade them farewell and started off with the men on the mountain journey.

After they had traveled for two days, they stopped and pitched a tent. Soon the two men began to whisper between themselves, and it wasn't long before the lad discovered their purpose. They had agreed to take all the boy's provisions for themselves; and so they did, leaving him only a bone and a few scraps of meat.

The farmer's son was very angry but, as it was impossible for him to fight these two big men, he was obliged to keep silent. When the rascals had finished their stolen meals, they lay down to sleep. But the lad was so disturbed that he could neither eat nor sleep.

After a while a brown dog came to the tent and, having sniffed around, lifted the flap with its nose. The boy threw the bone to the dog who snapped it up and disappeared. The dog had the most human expression the lad had ever seen and, since he couldn't sleep, he left the tent to look for this strange animal.

Then he saw a tall old man coming toward him followed by the brown dog.

The stranger greeted the boy kindly and asked him many questions which the lad answered modestly and well. At last he told the old man all about himself, and chiefly how matters stood with his companions. The man then offered him work as a day laborer on his farm, and the lad gladly consented. He took the horse and went away with the stranger while the two men remained sound asleep in the tent.

All that day and the following night they traveled together until they came to a little cottage in a valley. There were beautiful grounds and meadows around the cottage, but everything in the distance seemed to be covered by a dense fog.

The old man's daughter stood outside the cottage and welcomed the lad and her father. Then the man showed the boy the storehouse where a bed was made ready for him. He asked his daughter to bring food for the youth and to wait upon him carefully. All this she did most graciously, and when the lad went to bed, he slept soundly throughout the night.

The next morning the old man told the boy that he had chosen his work for the summer. There were large meadows thickly grown with grass which he had to finish mowing before the people made their autumn search for their sheep. The youth thought this would be a task far beyond his powers, but he said nothing.

Then the master gave him a good scythe and he bade his daughter rake up the hay. After this, he strongly warned the lad not to show any curiosity about the ways of his household.

And so the farmer's son cut grass every day and slept in the storehouse at night, yet he never saw anyone but the master and his beautiful daughter, nor was he aware of there being any other creature but the brown dog in the whole valley. He cut the grass and the girl raked the hay. Still there was one thing that astonished him above all others—as soon as the grass was cut and raked, it vanished!

The lad found his lonely life rather unusual, but not altogether uninteresting—especially because he found the girl's company so pleasant.

Before the summer ended, he finished his work, and the master came and thanked him for his labor. "Now it is time for you to go home so you will not be left behind by your two neighbors," said he. "They have remained in the tent where you left them until two weeks ago when they went north. Of course they found little work since the summer is almost over."

How the old man knew all this, the lad never discovered, nor did he ask any questions.

The man gave the boy his summer wages which included two casks of butter, two sheep, and liberal provisions for the journey. He brought the boy's horse and a comely gray of his own. "This old nag will carry the butter to your home," he said. "I myself will accompany you to the spot where we first met."

Before they were ready to leave, the master brought a horn and asked the lad to drink from it. The youth took a draught and suddenly felt stronger. Then the man bade him wrestle, but when they had wrestled a short while, the lad got the worst of it. So the old man told him to take another draught from the horn, and this time he wrestled a great deal better. But after taking a third draught, the youth wrestled long and powerfully.

The master smiled and said, "Now if you should encounter two strong men on your journey, you will have no trouble overcoming them."

Then the youth took leave of the beautiful young girl. He kissed her and mounted his horse, leading the gray nag by the reins. The old man walked by his side while the brown dog drove the sheep before them.

When they came to the place where they had first met, the man asked him to work again the following summer, which the boy promised to do. They appointed the same spot for their next meeting and bade one another farewell.

After the youth had traveled for a while, he met his old companions who were going south with little luck and meager wages. They welcomed him as though nothing had happened and asked where he had been all summer.

"That is no business of yours," the young man told them.

"We shall soon see," they said, "for you must share your wages with us."

"I'll do no such thing," replied the lad.

"We will let strength decide the matter," said the men.

The youth was quite ready for that as he was eager to punish them for their past thievery. So they all dismounted from their horses, and the two ruffians thought they'd easily take all the boy's wages away from him. But he quickly caught each of them by the hand and hurled them a long way off. They were badly bruised and found it difficult to get on their legs again—nor did they think of encountering this giant's strength for a second time. Then the young man continued his journey unmolested.

When he arrived at his home, he freed the gray horse, and off it went, followed by the brown dog. His parents were very glad to see him return from his labors so richly rewarded. They were amazed at the sheep he had brought them as they had never seen so large and fine a breed. But in spite of their questioning, the young man said very little about his travels or where he had dwelt during the summer.

He spent the next winter at home with his parents, and he was greatly admired by everyone in the district for his strength and diligence.

When summer came, the youth went away, and having reached the appointed place at the right time, he met his former master. They traveled to the cottage in the valley where everything was the same as the previous year. No one was to be seen but the old man's daughter who greeted him warmly.

After the youth had rested a while, the old man gave him the scythe. He then showed him the fields which had to be mowed during the same period of time as the summer before, only now they had grown much thicker. But the time passed quickly as the young man and girl worked and talked together. He cut the grass while she raked; and, once again, all the hay vanished after it had been raked.

The lad had grown so strong that he completed his labors a week earlier than the first summer. Then, as he sat in the storehouse thinking sadly about leaving the girl, the old man came to him and said, "I cannot help wondering how quickly you finished the work in spite of the time you spent talking with my daughter." And then he added, "It was quite clear that your joint labors were not irksome to either one of you."

This the youth could not deny, and the old man smiled. "I have twelve daughters, eleven of whom are already married. They each have a farm in this valley. But my twelfth daughter, whom you know, is unmarried and the youngest of them all. And I believe it is the wish of you both that you be joined in marriage."

The young man was very happy and he consented with all his heart to this arrangement.

Then the old man said, "You have done well in not asking questions about the strange way of life at this farm. And now I may tell you that there are really many people working here."

After this, the old man took a piece of glass from his pocket and bade the lad look into it. Then, to the boy's surprise, he saw a great and beautiful valley with twelve farms and many people engaged in haymaking. He also saw scattered herds of cattle and horses, and large flocks of magnificent sheep. And he saw, too, all the men and women who were working in the fields at the old man's own farm. But no sooner did he move the glass from his eyes than all vanished and looked as it had before.

"This is a secret valley!" said the boy in amazement.

"So it is," said the old man, "and so it shall remain."

The following day the young man and his betrothed prepared for the journey back to his parents' home, and the girl's father equipped them carefully. He gave them sixteen of his best sheep which the dog was to drive back for them. Besides these, he loaded the gray horse with many costly gifts and said that he would guide them as far as he had the previous summer.

Then they started off together until they reached the appointed spot where the old man took leave of them with a fatherly kiss and wished them luck and happiness. After this, the youth and the girl went homeward with the horse carrying its costly load and the dog driving the fine sheep.

When they arrived, the horse and the dog went back to the valley as before. The couple were gladly welcomed by the young man's parents. Within a few months they were married, and then there was great rejoicing, for the young man and the girl were admired by everyone in the parish.

The couple lived a long and happy life together. But no one in the district, besides these two, ever knew of the secret valley.

THE WISH
THAT
CAME TRUE

Francisco de Paula Capella

I N the early days of the Goths there lived a powerful knight who had built a castle with a moat and strong walls perched high on a mountain. His lands stretched for miles around, and his castle was protected by many guards. And thus secured from want and from attack, he was a happy man.

One winter's night, as he sat by the fire of huge logs, with the wind whistling, the rain falling, and the owls uttering their weird notes, a page entered and announced that a stranger at the castle gate was asking to be admitted.

"Let him come in," answered the lord. "On such a night as this none must be refused hospitality."

The page left and, shortly after, a man with a dark cloak and flowing white beard entered the room. His fine face, and great dignity at once commanded the knight's respect. He invited the stranger to sit at his table where the best of food was served to him.

"I do not know how to repay you for your goodness," said the stranger, "for I see that you are wealthy and have the most exotic food at your table and gold and silver in your abode. I can only thank you for the kindness you have shown me."

"You think I am happy," answered the lord, "because you see gold and silver glisten around me. Yet, since yesterday, I have been overwhelmed with sadness. I have in my room a steel mirror, and as I looked at my reflection I saw white hairs in my beard and upon my head. This has thrown me into despair, for white hairs mean the coming of old age, and old age means death. I want to live forever so as not to abandon such wealth and happiness."

"Your desire is folly," said the stranger.

"That may be," answered the knight, "but when I consider that I must die, and this castle and these lands must become the property of others, I am beside myself with grief. It seems but a brief time that I can enjoy them."

"You are still young, my good lord, and have, perhaps, thirty years of life before you."

"Thirty years! What is that compared to eternal life! I would give half of all I possess never to die."

"Your wish is madness," replied the stranger. "If you had eternal life, you yourself would beg to end it."

"That I would never do," said the knight.

For a long while the stranger was silent; his eyes looked far away as though he were in a trance. And when at last he spoke, it was the merest whisper. "One day you will discover the folly of your wish. But for now, you shall have what you want. Do you see this green wood?" and he pointed to a log near the hearth. "Take it and hide it away so it shall not be burned. You will live on as long as it remains unburned."

"Life! Life!" cried the knight, radiant with joy, and he snatched up the log and hurried from the room.

When he returned, the stranger had disappeared, but the knight was too excited to notice. "No one will ever find the log where I have hidden it," he thought, "and it will never be burned. This castle and land will remain mine. I shall see generation after generation, and shall be the king of the world because I will never die."

And at last the Gothic knight retired to his room. The castle hall was left in darkness as the glow of the embers was veiled by the ashes. Only the wind howled and the cries of the owls resounded among the crags and clefts of the mountain.

Centuries passed; the knight lived on and on. Gradually he became little more than a skeleton who sat miserably before his fireside, winter and summer. And when his trembling hands stretched out to catch the warmth of the fire, they seemed almost transparent.

His castle, once magnificent and strong, was now gray and tottering from the ravages of time. Its only habitable rooms afforded shelter to an old caretaker and the ancient knight himself.

"Who is he?" asked the occasional visitors whose curiosity had brought them to the castle.

"Nobody knows," said the old caretaker, "for he speaks an ancient language which no one can understand."

When people addressed the knight, he replied in his own strange tongue and pointed with tremulous fingers to the roof. But his words were meaningless to them, and the knight could only shake his head and relapse into his usual attitude of despair.

One day a scholar was led by his love of antiquity to visit the castle. He was versed in the lore of the past and learned in ancient languages.

The caretaker showed the scholar all the curiosities of the castle and lastly, the most remarkable of all, the aged unknown whom no one could remember ever having been younger than he appeared at the present time.

The scholar approached the knight and asked who he was, and the knight answered in his own language.

The scholar was astonished. "Why, you speak the Gothic tongue!" said he.

The poor man uttered a cry of joy at hearing his native speech. "At last," he cried, "I have found someone who understands me. . . . Please tell the caretaker to go up to the attic yonder. There, in the left-hand corner, covered with stones, he will find a log. Tell him to bring it down and burn it in the fire."

"That is a strange request, my good sir," said the scholar.

"So it may seem," said the knight, "but I implore you to do as I ask."

The scholar translated the knight's words to the caretaker who went up to the attic at once.

"I see you have found it," said the scholar when he returned.

"Yes," said the caretaker, "but the log was so well hidden that no one would have discovered it, for it was in the most ancient part of the castle."

Meanwhile the knight gestured to the caretaker to put the log upon the fire, and the good man, seeing his eagerness, hastened to comply. The log, which had been drying for centuries, began to burn like tinder.

Then the aged knight smiled with pleasure. He embraced the scholar and recounted his history, beginning with the night of the stranger's visit.

". . . And so I have lived to see my castle crumble to decay and my lands taken from me. When my own generation disappeared, I was no longer known to anyone. No visitor understood my native tongue, for even the language of the country had changed.

"I wanted to live forever so that I could enjoy more than others, and few men have been as miserable and lonely as I. I longed for death and kept telling people to fetch the log and burn it. But no one paid me any heed, and I was too decrepit to get it myself. And so my days have been endless until you came to save me.

"When I begged for eternal life, the stranger told me that my wish was folly. 'Ah, how truly he spoke! How seldom does man know what is best for him."

The scholar listened in amazement as the knight finished his story. The ancient man's face looked peaceful while the fire burned. And when, at last, the dry log smoldered into ashes, the Gothic knight was able to close his eyes forever.

EL ENANO

Charles Finger

EVERYONE disliked El Enano, who lived in the forest, because he always lay hidden in dark places, and when woodmen passed he jumped out on them and beat them and took their dinners from them. He was a squat creature, yellow of skin and snag-toothed and his legs were crooked, his arms were crooked, and his face was crooked. There were times when he went about on all fours, and then he looked like a great spider for he had scraggly whiskers that hung to the ground and looked like legs. At other times he was in the mood to make himself very small like a little child, and then he was most horrible to see, for his skin was wrinkled and his whiskers hung about him like a ragged garment.

Yet all of that the people might have forgiven and he might have been put up with, were it not for some worse tricks. What was most disliked was his trick of walking softly about a house in the night time while the people were inside, suspecting nothing, perhaps singing and talking. Seeing them thus, El Enano would hide in the shadows until someone went for water to the spring, then out he would leap, clinging fast to the hair of the boy or man and beating, biting, scratching the while. Being released, the tortured one would of course run to reach the house, but El Enano would hop on one leg behind, terribly fast, and catch his victim again just as a hand was almost laid on the door latch. Nor could an alarm be raised, because El Enano cast a spell of silence, so that, try as one would, neither word nor shout would come.

Then there was his other evil trick of hiding close to the ground and reaching out a long and elastic arm to catch a boy or girl by the ankle. But that was not worse than his habit of making a noise like hail or rain. When the people in the house heard this, they would get up to close a window, and there, looking at them from the dark but quite close to their faces, would be the grinning Enano holding in his hands his whiskers that looked like a frightening curtain, his eyes red and shining like rubies. That was very unpleasant indeed, especially when a person was alone in the house. Nor was it much better when he left the window, for he would hop and skip about the house yard for hours, screaming and howling and throwing sticks and stones. So, wherever he was there was chill horror.

One day, a good old woman who lived alone went with her basket to gather berries. El Enano saw her and at once made himself into a little creature no larger than a baby and stretched himself on a bed of bright moss between two trees, leafless and ugly. He pretended to be asleep, though he whimpered a little as a child does when it has a bad dream.

The good old woman was short-sighted but her ears were quick, and hearing the soft whimper she found the creature and took it in her arms. To do that bent her sadly, for Enano when small was the same weight as when his full size.

"Oh, poor thing," she said. "Someone has lost a baby. Or perhaps some wild creature has carried the tender thing from its home. So, lest it perish I will take care of it, though to be sure, a heavier baby I never held."

The dame had no children of her own and, though poor, was both willing and glad to share what she had with any needy creature. Gently she took it home and having put dry sticks on the fire she made a bed of light twigs which she covered with a mat of feathers. Then she bustled about, getting bread and milk for supper for the little one, feeling happy at heart because she had rescued the unhappy creature from the dismal forest.

At first she was glad to see the appetite of the homeless thing, for it soon finished the bread and milk and cried for more.

"Bless me! It must be half starved," she said. "It may have my supper." So she took the food she had set out for herself and El Enano swallowed it as quickly as he had swallowed the first bowl of food. Yet still he cried for more. Off then to the neighbors she went, borrowing milk from this one, bread from that, rice from another, until half the children of the village had to go on short rations that night. The creature devoured all that was brought and still yelled for more, and the noise it made was ear-splitting. And as it ate and felt the warmth, it grew and grew.

"Santa Maria!" said the dame. "What wonderful thing is this? Already it is no longer a baby, but a grown child. Almost it might be called ugly, but that, I suppose, is because it was motherless and lost. It is all very sad." Then, because she had thought it ugly she did the more for it, being sorry for her thoughts, though she could not help nor hinder them. As for the creature itself, having eaten all in the house, it gave a grunt or two, turned heavily on its side and went to sleep, snoring terribly.

Next morning matters were worse, for El Enano was stretched out on the floor before the fire, his full size, and seeing the dame he called for food, making so great a noise that the very windows shook and his cries were heard all over the village. So to still him, and there being nothing to eat in the house, the good old woman went out and told her tale to the neighbors, asking their help and advice, and to her house they all went flocking to look at the strange creature. One man, a stout-hearted fellow, told El Enano that it was high time for him to be going, hearing which, the ugly thing shrieked with wicked laughter.

"Well, bring me food," it said, looking at the man with red eyes. "Bring me food, I say, and when I have eaten enough I may leave you. But bring me no child's food, but rather food for six and twenty men. Bring an armadillo roasted and a pig and a large goose and many eggs and the milk of twenty cows. Nor be slow about it for I must amuse myself while I wait, and it may well be that you will not care for the manner of my amusement."

Indeed, there was small likelihood of any one there doing that, for his amusement was in breaking things about
the house, the tables and benches, the pots and the jars,
and when he had made sad havoc of the woman's house he
started on the house next door, smashing doors and windows, tearing up flowers by the roots, chasing the milk
goats and the chickens, and setting dogs to fight. Nor did
he cease in his mischief until the meal was set out for him,
when he leaped upon it and crammed it down his throat
with fearful haste, leaving neither bone nor crumb.

The people of the village stood watching, whispering
one to another behind their hands, how they were shocked
at all that sight, and when at last the meal was finished, the
stout-hearted man who had spoken before stepped forward. "Now, sir!" said he to El Enano, "seeing that you
have eaten enough and more than enough, you will keep
your word, going about your business and leaving this
poor woman and us in peace. Will you?"

"No. *No.* NO!" roared El Enano, each No being louder
than the one before it.

"But you promised," said the man.

What the creature said when answering made nearly everyone there faint with horror. It said:

"What I promised was that I would leave when I had
eaten enough. I did not—"

The bold man interrupted then, saying, "Well, you have
eaten enough."

"Ah yes, for one meal," answered the cruel Enano.
"But I meant that I would leave when I have eaten enough
for always. There is tomorrow and tomorrow night. There
is the day after that and the next day and the next day.
There are to be weeks of eating and months of eating and
years of eating. You are stupid people if you think that I

shall ever have eaten enough. So I shall not leave. No. *No*. NO!"

Having said that, the creature laughed in great glee and began to throw such things as he could reach against the walls, and so, many good things were shattered.

Now for three days that kind of thing went on, at the end of which time the men of the place were at their wits' ends to know what to do, for almost everything eatable in the village had gone down the creature's throat. Sad at heart, seeing what had come to pass, the good old woman went out and sat down to weep by the side of a quiet pool. It seemed to her to be a hard thing that what she had done in kindness had ended thus, and that the house she had built and loved and kept clean and sweet should be so sadly wrecked and ruined. Her thoughts were broken by the sound of a voice, and turning she saw a silver-gray fox sitting on a rock and looking at her.

"It is well enough to have a good cry," he said, "but it is better to be gay and have a good laugh."

"Ah! Good evening, Señor Zorro," answered the dame, drying her tears. "But who can be gay when a horrible creature is eating everything? Who can be otherwise than sad, seeing the trouble brought on friends?" The last, she added, being one of those who are always saddened by the cheerlessness of others.

"You need not tell me," said the fox. "I know everything that has passed," and he put his head a little sideways like a wise young dog and seemed to smile.

"But what is there to do?" asked the dame. "I am in serious trouble indeed. This wild one says that he will not stir until he has had enough to eat for all his life, and certainly he makes no move to go away."

"The trouble is that you give him enough and not too much," said the fox.

"Too much, you say? We have given him too much already, seeing that we have given him all that we have," said the old dame a little angrily.

"Well, what you must do is to give him something that he does not like. Then he will go away," said the fox.

"Easier said than done," answered the old woman with spirit. "If we gave him something that he did not like, then he would eat ten times more to take the bad taste away. Señor Zorro, with all your cleverness, you are but a poor adviser."

After that the fox thought a long while before saying anything, then coming close to the old woman and looking up into her face he said:

"Make your mind easy. He shall have enough to eat this very night, and all that you have to do is to see that your neighbors do as I say, nor be full of doubt should I do anything that seems to be contrary."

So the good old woman promised to warn her neighbors, knowing well the wisdom of the fox, and together they went to her house, where they found El Enano stretched out on the floor, looking like a great pig, and every minute he gave a great roar. The neighbors were both angry and afraid, for the creature had been very destructive that day. Indeed, he had taken delight in stripping the thatched roofs and had desisted only when the men of the place had promised to double the amount of his meal.

Not five minutes had the fox and the dame been in the house when the men of the place came in with things—with berries and armadillos, eggs and partridges, turkeys and bread and much fish from the lake. At once they set about cooking, while the women commenced to brew a great bowl of knot-grass tea. Soon the food was cooked and El Enano fell to as greedily as ever.

The fox looked at Enano for a while, then said:

"You have a fine appetite, my friend. What will there be for the men and the women and the children and for me to eat?"

"You may have what I leave, and eat it when I end," said El Enano.

"Let us hope then that our appetites will be light," said the fox.

A little later the fox began to act horribly, jumping about the room and whining, and calling the people lazy and inhospitable.

"Think you," he said, "that this is the way to treat a visitor? A pretty thing indeed to serve one and let the other go hungry. Do I get nothing at all to eat? Quick. Bring me potatoes and roast them, or it will be bad for all of you. The mischief I do shall be ten times worse than any done already."

Knowing that some plan was afoot the people ran out of the house and soon came back with potatoes, and the fox showed them how he wanted them roasted on the hearth. So they were placed in the ashes and covered with hot coals and when they were well done the fox told everyone to take a potato, saying that El Enano, who was crunching the bones of the animals he had eaten, would not like them. But all the while the men were eating, the fox ran from one to another whispering things, but quite loud enough for Enano to hear. "Hush!" said he. "Say nothing. El Enano must not know how good they are and when he asks for some, tell him that they are all gone."

124

"Yes. Yes," said the people, keeping in with the plan. "Do not let Enano know."

By this time El Enano was suspicious and looked from one man to another. "Give me all the potatoes," he said.

"They are all eaten except mine," said the fox, "but you may taste that." So saying he thrust the roasted potato into the hands of Enano and the creature crammed it down its throat at once.

"Ha! It is good," he roared. "Give me more. More. MORE."

"We have no more," said the fox very loud, then, quite softly to those who stood near him, he added, "Say nothing about the potatoes on the hearth," but loudly enough for El Enano to hear, though quite well he knew that there were none.

"Ah! I heard you," roared El Enano. "There are potatoes on the hearth. Give them to me."

"We must let him have them," said the fox, raking the red-hot coals to the front.

"Out of the way," cried El Enano, reaching over the fox and scooping up a double handful of hot coals, believing them to be potatoes. Red hot as they were he swallowed them and in another moment was rolling on the floor, howling with pain as the fire blazed in his stomach. Up he leaped again and dashed out of the house to fling himself by the side of the little river. The water was cool to his face and he drank deep, but the water in his stomach turned to steam, so that he swelled and swelled, and presently there was a loud explosion that shook the very hills, and El Enano burst into a thousand pieces.

THE STORY
OF
O-TEI

Lafcadio Hearn

A long time ago, in the Japanese province of Echizen, there lived a man called Nagao Chōsei. Nagao was the son of a physician, and was educated for his father's profession. At an early age he had been betrothed to a girl called O-Tei, the daughter of one of his father's friends. Both families had agreed that the wedding should take place as soon as Nagao had finished his studies.

But the health of O-Tei proved weak, and in her fifteenth year she was attacked by a fatal illness. When she became aware that she must die, she sent for Nagao to bid him farewell.

As he knelt at her bedside, she said to him, "Nagao-Sama, we were promised to each other from the time of our childhood, and we were to have been married at the end of this year. But now I am going to die. The gods know what is best for us. If I could live for some years longer, I would only cause trouble and grief to others. With this frail body, I could not be a good wife. Therefore, even to wish to live, for your sake, would be very selfish. I am quite resigned to die, and I want you to promise that you will not grieve. Besides, I want to tell you that I think we shall meet again."

"Indeed we shall meet again," Nagao answered earnestly. "And in that Pure Land there will be no pain of separation."

"Nay, nay!" she responded softly, "I meant not the Pure Land. I believe that we are destined to meet again in this world—although I shall be buried tomorrow."

Nagao looked at her wonderingly, and saw her smile at his wonder. She continued in her gentle, dreamy voice, "Yes, I mean in this world, in your own present life, Nagao-Sama, if you wish it. Only for this to happen, I must be born a girl again and grow up to womanhood. So you will have to wait fifteen or sixteen years; that is a long time. But, my promised husband, you are now only nineteen years old."

Eager to soothe her dying moments, he answered, "To wait for you were no less a joy than a duty. We have been pledged to each other for the time of seven existences."

"But you doubt?" she questioned, watching his face.

"My dear one," he answered, "I doubt whether I will know you in another body, under another name—unless you can tell me of a sign or token."

"That I cannot do," she said. "Only the gods and the Buddha know how and where we shall meet. But I am sure—very, very sure—that, if you are not unwilling to receive me, I shall be able to come back to you. Remember these words of mine."

She ceased to speak, and her eyes closed. She was dead.

Nagao had truly loved O-Tei, and his grief was deep. He had a tablet made inscribed with her name, and he placed it in the household shrine. Every day he set offerings before it.

He thought a great deal about the strange things that O-Tei had said to him just before her death. And, in the hope of pleasing her spirit, he wrote a solemn promise to wed her if she could ever return to him in another body. This written promise he sealed with his seal, and placed in the shrine beside the mortuary tablet of O-Tei.

Nevertheless, as Nagao was an only son, it was necessary that he should marry. He soon found himself obliged to yield to the wishes of his family, and to accept a wife of his father's choosing.

After his marriage he continued to set offerings before the tablet of O-Tei, and he never failed to remember her with affection. But by degrees her image became dim in his memory, like a dream that is hard to recall. And the years went by.

During those years many misfortunes came upon him. His parents died—then his wife and only child. And so he found himself alone in the world. He abandoned his desolate home and set out on a long journey in the hope of forgetting his sorrows.

•

One day, in the course of his travels, he arrived at Ikao, a mountain village famed for its warm springs and beautiful scenery. In the village inn at which he stopped, a young girl came to wait upon him. At the first sight of her face, he felt his heart leap as it had never leaped before. So strangely did she resemble O-Tei that he pinched himself to make sure that he was not dreaming. As she went and came, bringing fire and food or arranging his chamber her every attitude and motion revived in him some gracious memory of the girl to whom he had been pledged in his youth.

At last he spoke to her, and she responded in a soft, clear voice the sweetness of which saddened him with the memory of other days.

Then, in great wonder, he questioned her, saying, "Elder Sister, so much do you look like a person whom I knew long ago that I was startled when you first entered this room. Pardon me, therefore, for asking what is your native place, and what is your name?"

Immediately—and in the unforgotten voice of the dead —she answered, "My name is O-Tei, and you are Nagao Chōsei, my promised husband. Seventeen years ago I died. Then in writing you made a promise to marry me if ever I could come back to this world. You sealed that written promise with your seal, and you put it in the shrine beside the tablet inscribed with my name. Therefore I came back . . ."

As she uttered these last words, she fell unconscious.

•

Nagao married her, and the marriage was a happy one. But at no time afterwards could she remember what she had told him in answer to his question at the inn. Neither could she remember anything of her previous existence. The memory of her former birth—mysteriously kindled in that moment of their meeting—had again become obscured, and so thereafter remained.

THE
TERRIBLE
STRANGER

Robert M. Hyatt

WINTER it was, and the night was drawn down cold and dark above the white ground. The chariot tracks were deep as a man's arm. The raw wind swept across the Plain of Macha, howling spitefully around the Royal House. It beat upon doors and windows, screaming away into the night.

Inside, all was light and warmth. The glow of blazing logs reddened the walls and glimmered in the silver and bronze of the ornaments that adorned them. The smell of burning wood was in the air, and the voices of poets and of harps drifted from the king's chamber. The huge Warriors' Hall was a happy place this night, where a group of Knights of the Red Branch of Ulster had drawn their chairs of carved yew wood close to the fire.

Wonderful peace and contentment there was over them

all—or, at any rate, contentment—for it had been a good year that was coming to an end. They talked of their victories, and of the vastness of the herds and the richness of the crops of Ulster. And they didn't fail to mention how all the power and glory of the kingdom was a credit to themselves.

Suddenly the noise of their voices ceased. And it wasn't the music that stopped them, either; nor yet the door that burst open with a great noise; nor even the big swirl of snow that blew in at them and kept whirling around the room, as if it had life in it. No, it was the terrible figure they saw standing there that put the silence on them—a tall man, big and awkward and ugly, with stooped shoulders and ravenous yellow eyes and a scraggly beard the color of peat. He had an old cowhide wrapped about him, and in his hand he held an enormous ax.

Loegaire Buadach, a big man with reddish-yellow hair, turned and faced him. "What do you want?" he demanded.

The stranger glowered at him. "I am looking for a man," he rumbled, and his voice seemed to come from far down in the cowhide.

"A man shouldn't be hard to find," said Loegaire, "not here." And he looked down at himself proudly. "Who are you?"

"Uath," answered the stranger.

"H'm! Well, what sort of man is it you want?"

Uath plucked a hair from his beard and dropped it on the gleaming edge of his ax where it fell in two pieces.

"The man I want," he said, "is the kind that is hard to find. But I don't know that there is a better one when he *is* found. And that is the kind who will keep an agreement."

Dubtach spoke up at that, a gloomy man with a fearsome voice. "You would have to leave this kingdom to find one who wouldn't," he growled. "An Ulsterman keeps his word."

Uath looked around the hall, and his eyes seemed to see into all the dark corners, even up into the black beams overhead.

"That is all I want," he said, "just the keeping of an agreement."

"What a pity Cuchulain is not here," said Fergus mac Roich. "He is a great lad for keeping his word. There are not many like Cuchulain and me. What sort of an agreement do you want kept?"

"This," replied Uath. "I am looking for a man who will keep this agreement with me: he is to cut off my head tonight, and I to cut off his head tomorrow night."

"You give him all the advantage," said Fergus.

"Advantage or no advantage," Uath growled, "that is the agreement."

"Cuchulain would like that," said Dubtach, "anything that had cutting off heads in it. He would keep his agreement, too, if he were here. Not but it is a queer enough one."

"It is the one I want," Uath mumbled. "Where is this Cuchulain?"

Loegaire Buadach got up. "Cuchulain is away now, but he is not the only man that keeps his word," said he, and he flung off his purple cloak. "Neither Cuchulain nor any man is the equal of myself. I am the Winner of Battles. Is there a single warrior in all Ireland that ever got the better of me? Is there one who can compare with me? Are there any ten men who are half as good as I am? Are there? You say you want me to cut off your head?"

"Mine, tonight," Uath said solemnly, "yours, tomorrow night. That is the agreement, if you are ready to make it."

"Where is my sword?" Loegaire shouted. "Someone fetch me my sword!"

"You may have the ax," said Uath.

"But what will you defend yourself with?"

"There is to be no defending ourselves. That is the agreement."

Loegaire took the ax. "We might as well go ahead. I don't mind telling you that you are spoiling a good deal of my pleasure in refusing to defend yourself. Would you want me to cut it off as you stand, or would you prefer . . ."

"You can please yourself," said Uath.

"You're very accommodating," Loegaire said politely. He felt the blade of the ax. "This is certainly a grand edge. If it is all the same with you, let someone get a block of wood. You might as well be comfortable."

So a block of wood was brought, and Uath knelt down and stretched his neck across it.

"I will cut off your head tomorrow night," he rumbled in his thunderous voice.

"Aye," said Loegaire, and he winked at Dubtach who had drawn his chair close and was watching very earnestly. Then Loegaire swung the ax high in the air, gave it a couple of twirls, and brought it down on Uath's neck with a mighty stroke that sent the head bounding off into a corner. There it lay with its eyes catching the light of the fire and flickering yellow flames. A log fell over in the fire so that a sudden flare shone full on Uath's body.

"It will be no easy matter for *him* to cut off your head tomorrow," remarked Dubtach.

"When *I* cut off heads," Loegaire snorted, "they're off." And he glared defiantly about him.

"You may give me the ax now," said a voice. It was a tired-sounding voice, and not as strong as the voices of most of the Ulstermen; but there was something very familiar about it. Loegaire looked around quickly to see who was speaking, but there wasn't a sound out of any of the warriors.

"My ax!" repeated the voice.

Loegaire spun around, and there was the body of Uath getting up from its knees. It stood for a moment in a half-puzzled sort of way. Then it seemed to make up its mind, and off it walked to where the head was lying. It picked up the head and tucked it under an arm. That seemed to make Uath feel better for, now that he had collected himself again, he came over to Loegaire briskly, took his ax, and started for the door.

"Tomorrow night, yours," said Uath's head from under his arm. Then he pulled the old cowhide around him and lumbered out into the darkness.

Loegaire Buadach, the Battle-Winner, was filled with terror. He sat down on the block of wood that Uath had finished with only a moment before, and he could hear the beating of his own heart.

"Never in all my life have I seen anyone do a thing like that!" said Dubtach.

"I wonder where he comes from," interrupted the warrior, Scel. "He can't be human!"

"What Loegaire is wondering," said Dubtach, "is whether Uath will really come back tomorrow night."

Then Loegaire looked down and saw what he was sitting on. He bounded to his feet with a shout, "I've been cheated."

137

"Cheated?" asked Dubtach. "How is that?"

"What business had he picking up his head again?" Loegaire yelled, striding rapidly up and down the room. "Cheated!" he roared. "That's what I've been. A man has no right to pick up his head once it has been chopped off."

"Perhaps he isn't a man at all," said Scel.

But Loegaire wasn't listening. He felt the back of his own neck, and all the terror and anger went out of him, leaving only sorrow. "I never could do a thing like that," he said. "I never could." He shook his head dejectedly. "Not but what it is a fine thing to be able to do. And now, what a fix I'm in!" He gave a great sigh. "Ah, well," said he, "I'm a man who keeps his agreements at any rate." And with that he went out.

But when the next night came, there wasn't a sign of Loegaire Buadach, the Battle-Winner. There was a fire blazing in the huge fireplace, and there was Fergus mac Roich sitting in front of it; and there was Scel and Dubtach, and ever so many others of the great fighting men of Ulster. But not a sign was there of Loegaire Buadach.

A great deal of talk there was, too, about him not appearing. And right in the middle of it all who should arrive but Conall Cernach, the Victorious. He was a big stout man with fair hair that was like a bushel-basket on top of his head.

Fergus nodded to him. "Ah, Conall, so it's you, is it? And have you seen Loegaire?"

"I have," replied Conall. "His chariot was going like the wind. But he kept waving in this direction, so I knew I must be wanted here. He yelled something about Cuchulain being our greatest champion . . ."

But Conall's words were interrupted by the door bursting open behind him. There stood Uath, with his head back on his shoulders and his yellow eyes looking hungrier than ever. His old cowhide was pulled around him, and his ax hung awkwardly in his hand.

Conall turned on him. "Who are you?" he demanded.

"I am a man who keeps his agreements," said Uath. "Are you?"

"Am I?" roared Conall. "Am I, indeed? Am I not the scourge of our enemies and the hope of our friends?"

"It is a good thing you are," said Uath, "for if that is the truth, maybe I could make an agreement with you and have you keep it."

"Keep it!" shouted Conall. "Of course I would keep it. Am I not the greatest in all Ulster? Why, for one little pebble from the ground I would cut off your head this very moment!"

"That is the agreement I would make with you," said Uath.

"What agreement?"

"You to cut off my head tonight, and I to cut off yours tomorrow night. Would you keep that agreement?"

Conall drew his sword with a grand flourish.

"Would I?"

"I am to cut off your head tomorrow night," Uath warned him.

"So you are!" Conall Cernach laughed as he whirled his great sword in the air and brought it across Uath's neck like a flash of light.

"Hah!" sneered Conall. "He'll be no trouble to anyone now." And he turned his back and started to walk off. But he hadn't gone far before he noticed the queer hush that was upon everyone. He turned and saw Uath's body getting up on its knees.

"You could have used my ax," said Uath's head, "only you were in such a hurry." And Uath's body picked up the head and put it carefully under its arm and walked out. With a slow sort of dignity he walked, too. It was easy to see that Uath didn't altogether like the way he had been hurried.

"Tomorrow night, yours," said the gory head.

Conall Cernach, the Victorious, one of the greatest of all Knights of the Red Branch, sat down as if his knees had been cut from under him. Every single hair in his bushy beard was standing as straight as a young pine tree.

When the next night came, there was no sign of either Loegaire Buadach, the Battle-Winner, or of Conall Cernach, the Victorious. Back came Uath, the same as before, with his yellow eyes gleaming, his old cowhide wrapped about him, and his ax in his hand. There was a great host of knights gathered around the fireplace, but when Uath glowered around at them, there was nothing but silence.

"Well?" said Uath in his rumbling voice.

"Aye," said Fergus mac Roich. "It *is* a cold night, for a fact."

"Never mind the cold," snapped Uath. "What about the agreement I made?"

Suddenly the door burst open, and into the room bounded a small, dark man with a gorgeous purple cloak about him.

"Cuchulain himself!" exclaimed Dubtach.

There stood Cuchulain, eyeing them all. His sword was in his hand—his sword with its hilt of gold, its point that would bend back to the hilt, and its blade that would cut a man in half so swiftly that the one half wouldn't know when the other half had gone from it.

"Look here, Cuchulain," said Fergus, "they tell me a party of Connachtmen has been seen over beyond Coolgair. Wouldn't it be a good thing for you to run them out?"

"Conall Cernach has gone after them," answered Cuchulain.

"Conall Cernach?"

"Aye. I met him, and he told me that some stranger was here."

Uath walked in front of him. "It was I," he said.

"It was, was it?" shouted Cuchulain. "Defend yourself then!" And he whirled his great sword around his head.

Uath leaned on his ax and stood there facing Cuchulain. "I have no need for defense," said he, "so long as you'll keep your agreements." At that a red flush came to Cuchulain's face and his cheeks glowed, and his eyes shone with the warrior's flame that would come upon him in moments of anger.

"Never," he shouted, "has an agreement of mine gone unkept. Never have I turned my back on an enemy or on a friend, although whole armies avoid me. Forty heads with one stroke of my sword can I . . ."

"Cuchulain!" cried Fergus mac Roich, "I wouldn't. . ."

"What do I care whether you would or not?" Cuchulain whirled on Fergus. "Forty heads with a single stroke . . ."

"It is an agreement with you that I want," interrupted Uath, "if you'll keep it."

"Keep it?" roared Cuchulain, who was on fire with

wrath. "Keep it? I'll keep any agreement with anyone anywhere. Take your ax and defend yourself!"

"There's no need for that," replied Uath softly. "You can cut off my head now if you'll agree to let me cut off yours tomorrow night. That's all."

Before anyone could say another word, there was a flash like that of lightning. And there was Cuchulain letting the point of his sword come to rest on the ground, and there was Uath standing in front of him swaying on his feet as if a strong wind had struck him. He put one hand up to his neck, did Uath, and he felt it; yet he could feel nothing amiss. But when he tried to turn his head, it rolled off his shoulders and tumbled to the ground.

"O Cuchulain," groaned Fergus mac Roich, "how often have I warned you about your hasty temper!"

Cuchulain looked from one to the other in great puzzlement at the way they were behaving—until he happened to glance down at the body of Uath, which was busy picking up its head. Cuchulain stood as if suddenly turned to stone.

Uath took the head and put it under his arm, as he had done twice before, although he seemed to be more tired than ever this time. His feet dragged as he walked toward the door, and his hand shook, and he nearly dropped his ax as he drew the old cowhide around him.

"Tomorrow night, your head," said Uath's head as he went out.

"Will you look at what you have done," moaned Fergus.

"Maybe Uath will not come back," said Scel. "After all, a man can't go on getting his head cut off. There must be an end to it sometime. He'll wear out."

Cuchulain looked at them all in amazement. "It is the

first time I ever saw a man pick up his own head," he said, "and hundreds of heads have fallen at my feet."

"He has done it twice before."

"Twice before?"

"Aye! Loegaire Buadach and Conall Cernach cut off Uath's head, but neither of them came back for their part of the agreement. So there is no need of your . . ."

"I shall be here," said Cuchulain, and he drew his purple cloak around him and took a couple of steps toward the door. Then he stopped. "In fact, I'll stay here," he said.

"Now, Cuchulain, listen to me," began Fergus, "you didn't know how this was going to turn out. How could you? What right has a man to put his head back on him again after you cut it off so beautifully? And it *was* off. I couldn't have cut it off better myself."

Cuchulain waved him away. "It makes no difference," he said. "My agreement must be kept. I shall be here."

And he was, too, the very next night when Uath came in with his swirl of snow and the cold wind that caused everyone to move closer to the fire. Right in the center of Warriors' Hall Cuchulain stood, and never a move out of him, until Uath lumbered up to him with his old cowhide steaming in the warm air, and his yellow eyes burning as if there was a fire raging inside of him.

"So you're here!" said Uath.

"I am." Cuchulain's voice was very quiet, and there was no warrior's flame in him any more.

"Ah," said Fergus mac Roich, "this is a bad day that is come upon us. Why did it have to be himself that must be taken from us in all the greatness of his glory? Go and tell Conchobar the way things are, Scel."

So Scel went to the Royal Chamber and told the great

King Conchobar of the terrible things that had come to pass, and the king hurried to the hall, his full-moon face looking pale. For Scel had left nothing out, even in so hasty a telling of the story.

There they were then, all gathered in the Warriors' Hall, King Conchobar and a host of the greatest men of Ulster. Cuchulain stood sad and alone by a big block of wood. Uath stood at his side.

"O Cuchulain," lamented the king, "is there no way out?"

"There is not," answered Cuchulain, "though I wish there were." And he looked all around the great hall, with its glow of ruddy lights and its deep shadows and the great shields of silver and bronze hanging on the walls.

"There is no way out," he continued, "for when a man like me gives his word, that is the end of the matter."

Then he turned to Uath. "Is there anything keeping you?" he asked.

"There is not," said Uath, "unless it be the need of having you kneel down."

So Cuchulain knelt down and put his head across the block of wood, so that his neck was a fair invitation to the ax.

Uath watched him for a moment, then he walked all around him. "Ah!" said he thoughtfully. Then he took another walk in the other direction. "H'm!" said he.

Then Uath took the ax and ran his fingers along the edge of the blade. "It is sharp," he remarked, and his voice was as slow as a chariot being dragged over boulders. "Yet I wonder if it is sharp enough."

"Get on with what you're doing," Cuchulain ordered.

Uath let the ax drop to the ground with a thud, and he

stood there resting on the handle of it. "You would not want your head cut off with a blunt ax, would you?" he asked.

"What do I care? Get on with it!"

"But you ought to care," Uath warned. "It makes a great difference to a man, when getting his head cut off, whether the ax is sharp or not." He plucked a hair out of his beard and let it drop across the blade. "It is not dull," he said, as the hair divided itself. "Still, it is not so sharp." Then after considering for a while he said, "Well, maybe it will do. Still I don't know . . ."

"Will you get on?" thundered Cuchulain, his face getting redder than flames from his stooping and his thin lips beginning to twitch with anger. "How much longer must I wait?"

"Your sword was sharp when you used it on my neck," said Uath reproachfully. "But I think maybe the ax will do. Let me see now."

He raised the blade over his head and, as he raised it, he seemed to lengthen the way a shadow lengthens as the sun goes down. He raised it so high that the head of it struck the very beams of the roof; for a moment he held it there, poised, and the red light of the fire gleamed on its edge. Then Uath brought the ax down. In a mighty sweep it came, like a bolt falling out of the sky; only he turned the blade so that, instead of striking Cuchulain, it went past him, and the head of the ax struck the floor. It struck with such force that every man in the hall was shaken almost out of his seat.

Cuchulain remained kneeling by the block of wood, with his neck resting upon it and his head bowed at the farther side of it.

"Ah, well," said Uath, and his voice sounded a little less tired now, "you can get up, Cuchulain. You are the one man that kept his agreement with me; so you had better keep your head where it belongs, for it is too good a head to have rolling about on the ground. Indeed, there are few men who would rather have their necks severed than break their promises."

Uath looked around him with a slow look. "A kingdom," said he, "cannot last long if the agreements of its people are broken."

When he looked at Conchobar, the king was scowling angrily. But Fergus mac Roich was chuckling softly to himself.

Then Uath pulled his old cowhide around him. "I'm going back to Dun Curoi now," said he.

At these words, the silence was so great that even the logs in their blazing ceased to crackle; for everyone knew that the stranger was not Uath at all. He was Curoi, a man deeply versed in enchantment, famous throughout all Ireland for the magic spells he could cast.